SWEET LIES & KISSES

(THE UNDERCOVER FILES, #3)

JESSICA SORENSEN

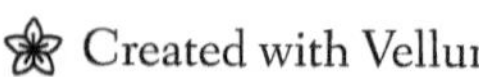 Created with Vellum

ONE

THE LAKE

I HAVE a feeling that everything I ever thought about my life is about to crumble. And I'm not sure if I can handle it. I've always been considered the strong one in my family, but that is mostly because I pretend to be. Deep down, I've always felt weak. And now, I'm about to find out how weak I am.

"The lines on my arms are starting to fade," I mumble to no one in particular.

Benton, who's driving the car, glances at my arms and a drop of relief sweeps across his face. "That's good. It means we're getting out of range of the scanner."

Out of range of the scanner? The words are another reminder of what just happened at my house, the beeping, the weird lines that appeared on my skin. Honestly, I'm not even positive what happened. I know Wilder said something about a scanner, but everything went crazy after that and no one really explained much to me, like why the veins on my arms turned dark or why Benton had a photo of me of when I was a kid.

"Out of range for what? That scanner? Because, what kind of scanner makes veins go dark? And why didn't any of you guys' veins turn dark?" A bit of annoyance creeps into my tone, but then I feel bad. "Sorry," I mutter, shaking my head. "No, actually, I don't know if I'm sorry or not."

Grrr ... sometimes it's so frustrating to be me. My instincts are to be nice, yet I'm so frustrated over the fact that Benton clearly has been keeping something from me. And do all the guys know more than they're letting on?

"You don't need to be sorry, sweetheart. You didn't do anything wrong," Benton tells me while raking his fingers through his dark hair that's shaved short on the sides. He keeps his other hand on the steering wheel, steering the car down the road, the sunlight flickering in his eyes.

"I know I didn't. I just don't know what's going on, and I'm frustrated and ..." I sigh, tucking a strand of my long, wavy brown hair behind my ear as I stare around at the fields lining the highway. "I don't know."

"Everything's going to be okay," Benton tries to reassure me.

But I don't believe him. How can I when it's pretty obvious he's been lying to me? And he hasn't told me much of anything, like where we're even going. I mean, initially, we were supposed to be going to the training pit, but now I'm not sure if that's still the plan.

"Where are we going?" I ask, aware that we're way out of the borders of Honeyton and heading in the direction of the hills that surround the town.

The last time I was out here was when I met Axel, when he tranquilized me. I should be uneasy because of that and with how vague the guys are acting. And I am. But I'm more concerned right now over the fact that, just a handful of minutes ago, my veins looked like they were about to burst out from under my skin.

"Somewhere safe," Wilder answers, scooting forward in the back seat. Strands of his chin-length, blond hair, the tips dyed blue, are in his eyes that are framed by eyelashes so long that he looks like he's wearing eyeliner. "Don't worry, princess; we're going to take care of you."

"God, please don't tell me you're going to start calling her princess now," Xavier mutters from the back seat. He's barely said anything since we took off, mostly just staring out the window.

"How do I know you guys will take care of me?" I state one of my worries aloud. "I don't really know you guys. And what I do know ..." I lift a shoulder, unsure of what else to say.

What I do know about the guys is pretty self-explanatory; that they work for a secret undercover program, as what I'm assuming are spies. Although no one has ever said the word "spies," it's pretty much what they seem like to me. And spies are known for being good liars. So, while these guys have been nice to me while I've been pretending to be Benton's girlfriend, who's to say if anything they've told me is true?

"No, you don't know us," Xavier says without glancing at me.

Out of all the guys, he's definitely the most intense, from the way he acts to the way he looks, constantly wearing leather jackets, biker boots, and his light brown hair is cut short enough to reveal a scar on the side of his head and the tattoos on the back of his neck.

"Xavier," Benton warns, glancing at him in the rearview mirror. "I thought we were past this."

By "past this," I think he means past Xavier hating me. He's acted that way since I was brought into the group. Well, except for on a few rare occasions, like when he let me eat his cereal and when we kissed in the parking lot. But the latter was all for show, so maybe he does still hate me.

Xavier narrows his eyes at Benton. "I'm not trying to be a dick. I'm simply stating a fact. She doesn't know us. How could she? She's known us for, like, what? A couple of days?"

"Well, she won't be able to get to know us if you keep treating her like shit." Benton holds Xavier's gaze in the rearview mirror, his gaze filled with a silent message that I can't quite decipher.

"I'm not treating her like crap," Xavier insists. "I was just pointing out that she doesn't know us very well. That's all." Shaking his head, he glances at me before turning back toward the window again. "I can't say two words without getting my ass chewed out."

Wilder offers me an amused smile. "You may not know us very well, but I think you're probably catching on that Xavier's the moody one." He smiles, and I crack the tiniest smile in return.

Xavier throws him a dirty look, parting his lips.

"Cut it out, you two," Benton cuts them off.

"And the wannabe boss has spoken," Wilder remarks with a roll of his eyes.

Xavier almost smiles but quickly stifles it and redirects his attention to the window. As he does, his eyes stray across me and, for the briefest moment, he appears puzzled. But it only lasts a moment before he returns to his normal, moody self.

And that's when I realize I'm just staring at him.

Awesome, Zhara, way to look like more of a freak than you already do.

I rotate around in my seat and fix my gaze out the window, unsure of what else to do since no one seems that eager to tell me anything.

The longer I sit in silence, the more worry stirs through me. I feel like I'm about to go crazy when my phone buzzes from inside my pocket.

I swiftly fish it out and breathe out in relief when I see the message is from Alexis, my non-identical twin sister who's been thrown into this undercover world, too. She's just with another group. I haven't spoken to her since Benton told me this information, and I've been beyond worried since this world is dangerous.

Alexis: Hey, so I can't call you right now, and I have to keep this message super vague. Since you're kind of in the same situation as me, I think you'll be able to figure out why. I just wanted to let you know that I'm safe, but I won't be able to go home for a while. From what I've heard, you might not either. Please be careful, okay? I know it doesn't always seem like it, but I do love you, Zee.

A faint smile touches my lips. It's been forever since she called me Zee. Since before our parents died. I miss the relationship we used to have and wonder if we'll ever be able to get back to that point in our lives. Then again, will we ever be able to return to our normal lives?

Alexis was fairly vague about what was going on, but my guess is she might be in a similar situation as me. The question is: why? Because our parents were once part of the undercover program? Who'd be after us because of that? Some drug lord? Rogues? What if it's someone from the undercover program? And if that's the case …

Benton, Wilder, and Xavier are part of the program.

I gulp as reality sets in. That I might not be safe right now.

My worry rises when Benton steers the car off the main highway and drives into the trees, out of sight of any civilization.

I'm about to ask where we're going when the trees open up into a small, flat area that leads to a cliff. And below the cliff is a lake.

"Why are we here?" I ask, sitting up straight in the seat, realizing no one ever told me where we're going.

No one answers as Benton parks the car in front of the cliff and shuts off the engine. Then he trades a look with Xavier and Wilder, and I get the most unsettling feeling that something awful is about to happen.

TWO
AN IRREVERSIBLE CHOICE

MY HANDS TREMBLE a bit as I contemplate reaching for the door handle and jumping out to make a run for it. Or maybe I should dig my phone out of my pocket and call for help? I'm not even sure if I should be panicking, though.

I'm so confused ...

"Relax," Benton tells me when he notes the—what I'm guessing—frantic look on my face. "Nothing bad is going to happen to you, I promise. We just need to be careful about what we say until we know for sure if we're completely out of range from everything."

I glance at the three of them, and then my gaze lands back on Benton. "I thought you said we were out of the range of the scanner?"

"Yeah, from the scanner the neighbor set off," Wilder explains, fiddling with a chain dangling from his black pants.

"Oh." I frown as puzzlement webs through me.

Benton slips the keys out of the ignition. "We should probably get in there so we can try to explain what's going on."

"Yeah, I know," Wilder says in agreement, seemingly worried about it.

I assess him, then Benton, noting how tense they both appear. "Why do you guys seem so tense?"

Benton rubs his lips together, his gaze flicking to me. "Because, once we take you into this place, everything will change."

"Everything already kind of has," I point out, scratching my arm. The skin is completely normal now.

Benton trades a quick look with the guys before focusing back on me. "This is different than that. What you're about to see ... Where we're going ..."

"It'll change the way you look at the world," Xavier finishes for him, his gaze locking with mine. "Everything you thought you knew is going to change, and you won't be able to go back, so you better make sure you want to do this."

I wrap my arms around myself. "Do I even have a choice?"

"You always have a choice." Benton stuffs the keys into his pocket. "We won't ever take that away from you."

I chew on my bottom lip, contemplating what he said. I've spent so many years trying to live up to my mom's expectations that the word *choice* almost feels foreign.

"And what if I say no, that I don't want to go to this place?" I ask. "Then what?"

Benton holds my gaze steadily. "Then we take you to a hotel and try to keep you safe there."

"Why don't you just do that now?" I ask, my confusion doubling.

Benton scratches the back of his neck then shrugs. "Because we don't want to leave you in the dark anymore."

"It's too risky." Wilder sweeps strands of hair out of his

eyes. "With everything going on, with everything that's happening to you, you need to know the truth."

"Does this have anything to do with why Benton has a photo of me from when I was younger?" I ask, chewing on my thumbnail.

Benton gives a small nod but doesn't make any effort to embellish.

And I could just leave it at that. Tell them to take me to a hotel, that I'll pretend like this strange day never happened. It seems like it might be easier. To go back to pretending everything is okay. Go back to being fake Zhara. But, after everything that's happened, I'm not sure I want to go back to being her. I'm not even sure I can.

So, mustering up every ounce of courage I have, I say. "I want to know everything. That's the choice I'm making."

The three of them nod but don't say anything, leaving me to wonder if they're upset or relieved by my choice.

THREE
AM I LIVING IN A HORROR MOVIE?

AFTER I MAKE MY DECISION, we all get out of the car. No one says a word as we meet in front of Benton's car, the breeze and the sound of waving water filling up the silence.

While it's the start of summer, the air up here is slightly chilly, and since I'm wearing shorts and a tank top, goosebumps sprout across my flesh. I wrap my arms around myself as I feel a shiver wanting to roll through me.

"Are you cold?" Benton asks, his gaze sweeping across me.

I shrug. "I always run a little bit colder. It's not a big deal, though."

"Yeah, Ridge mentioned that about you." Benton's brows knit as he contemplates something.

"We should probably get going," Wilder says, breaking the silence, wisps of his hair dancing in the wind. "It's kind of a long walk there."

Benton nods then spins toward the trees, his boots scuffing against the dirt as he hikes off. Wilder follows, grabbing ahold of my hand as he passes by me and pulling me with him. Xavier trails behind us.

As we endeavor into the trees, dirt starts to fill up my sandals, reminding me that I never really got to change my clothes before we left my house, which was the main point of us going there.

The deeper we get into the woods, the colder it gets as the shadows of the tree branches block out more and more sunlight. Eventually, I can't control the shivers coursing through my body.

"Oh, for the love of God," Xavier grumbles as he shucks off his jacket. "Here." He tries to hand the jacket to me, but I will my body to stop shaking.

"I'm fine."

He rolls his eyes and continues to hold the jacket out to me. "You're not fine. Your damn skin's turning blue."

I glance down at my arm and, sure enough, a bluish tint has spread across my skin.

"Jesus." Wilder skims his finger along the back of my hand. "No wonder your hand's freezing."

"I'm always kind of cold," I say again, feeling like a freak of nature.

"Yeah, I know, you said that, but still ..." He wavers for a beat then cups my hand between his, lifts it to his mouth, and then breathes warm breaths onto my skin.

While I appreciate the effort, I know enough about my body to understand this won't warm me up. Xavier's jacket might, though. But he seems like he's irritated at himself for trying to give it to me.

"Just take the damn jacket, Zhara," Xavier urges the jacket at me again.

When I just shake my head, he rolls his dark eyes.

"I'm not going to put it back, so just take the damn thing."

Sighing, I take the jacket from him with my free hand. "Thanks."

He gives an indifferent shrug before striding after Benton. Wilder breathes on my hand one more time before letting me go so I can slip the jacket on.

"I don't think Xavier likes me very much," I say as I slip my arms through the sleeves of the jacket.

"Nah." Wilder dismisses my statement with a flick of his wrist. "He's always like that."

I zip up the jacket. "Even to you guys?"

He gives a wavering nod. "When we first met him, yeah. Now he has his moments where he can be chill. But those are few and far between."

"Oh." My gaze drifts to where Xavier is striding up the path.

I want to know why he's like that, so closed off and angry. But I'm not about to ask Wilder to spill secrets to me about his friend. Maybe one day Xavier will decide to like me enough to talk to me. Then again, will I even be in these guys' world long enough for that to happen? I'm not sure.

I'm not sure about much of anything anymore.

And going from having my entire future mapped out to not knowing what's going to happen in the next few minutes is terrifying. I should run. Turn away and head back to the path that mapped my next five years. The old Zhara would have. But the new Zhara ...

I start walking forward again, heading after Xavier and Benton with Wilder by my side. We walk in silence for a bit, the sounds of twigs breaking filling up the quietness. Everyone seems content with that silence. Usually, I am, too. But the longer it goes on, the more I worry about what awaits for me ahead, what's going on with me, what secrets these guys are keeping from me. My mind starts racing so swiftly with worry that it starts to drive me mad.

"You seem restless," Wilder states as he pushes a tree branch out of our way.

"I'm just nervous," I admit. "And all this silence is making me think about the what-ifs." I shrug. "I'm kind of a worrier."

"Yeah, I get that," he says, and I assume he's referring to me, but then he adds, "I may not seem like it, but I worry a lot, too."

"Really?" I ask with a hint of doubt. "You seem so ... I don't know, laidback. Well, not as laidback as Jett."

"No one's as laidback as Jett," he stresses with a smile. "But Jett's only laidback all the time because he's stoned most of the time." He pushes another tree branch out of the way. "The only time he's not stoned is when he's working a job. Even then, I know he is sometimes, despite what he tells Benton."

"How does he keep a clear head to work then?" I wonder, hoping I don't sound naïve.

"It just kind of seems to work for him. Maybe because he's done it for so long?" He gives a shrug, the chain dangling from his belt loop jingling as he sidesteps around a rock blocking the path. "Honestly, we all wish he'd cut back. But you can't force someone to do that. They have to want to. And until Jett deals with"—he tenses—"stuff, he probably won't."

I want to ask what sort of stuff but don't want to seem nosy.

"Me, on the other hand," Wilder continues, dazzling me with a grin, "I've got the clearest head in the group."

"Really?" I question.

"Yes, really." He grins amusedly. "Why the doubt?"

I offer him an apologetic look, hoping I didn't offend him. "You just told me once that your head was full of a lot of things, that it was an artist's curse."

"True," he says, draping an arm around my shoulders. "I guess I have a cluttered clear head then."

"That literally makes no sense." Jackson suddenly steps out from the trees lining the side of the path.

I startle at his sudden appearance, nearly jolting out of my skin, and end up stumbling into Wilder.

Wilder steadies me. "Easy, princess. You don't need to be so jumpy."

"You're calling her princess now?" Jackson asks as he adjusts the tie around his neck, loosening it.

He's sporting his typical preppy look—a button-down shirt, jeans, and Converse sneakers. His blond hair is styled, wisps hanging into his eyes that always seem to sparkle with a hint of amusement. Well, except for when he's stressed out.

Honestly, up until I got to know him a little bit, I thought he was the sort of guy who was always unbothered, but then I learned that, if someone he knows is hurt or hurting, he gets more stressed out than your average person.

"Seriously, come up with something more original," Jackson continues as he strolls up to us with his hands tucked inside his back pockets.

"Zhara likes it," Wilder replies. "So, why does it bother you?"

"It doesn't bother me. I'm just saying that, with how much you brag about being so original all the time, you'd think you'd be able to come up with a more unique nickname for her."

Jackson flashes Wilder a smirk, but it fades when his gaze shifts to me.

"How are you doing?" Concern masks his expression.

"I'm fine," I automatically say.

"Fine is a replacement word," he replies, walking beside me as we continue down the path and farther into the woods.

I sigh, knowing he's right and knowing I use the word a lot. "I know."

His brow arches. "So, then how are you really feeling?"

"I'd like to know that, too," Wilder says, pulling me closer to his side.

I glance between the two guys, wondering why this is so hard for me—to admit how I really feel. Perhaps because I've spent so many years covering up my emotions and pretending everything was perfect.

"Honestly," I say, "I'm kind of freaked out. With what happened at the house ... and those lines appearing on my arm ..." I swallow hard. "Plus, you guys are keeping stuff from me, and I can tell it's bad."

Jackson gives me a sympathetic look. "Being freaked out is totally understandable, but I promise—we all promise—that nothing bad will happen to you."

He may believe what he said, but after everything that's happened, I know that's something he can't control. Still, I force a smile on my lips, being the polite Zhara because, truthfully, I'm too damn tired and worried to do anything else.

And that worry only skyrockets when we come to a stop, not just in the middle of the forest but also in front of a small log cabin.

The windows are covered with curtains, the wraparound

porch is partially collapsed, and an old shed is located just behind it.

"This looks like a place out of a horror movie," I mumble tensely.

The corners of Jackson's lips twitch upward. "That's kind of the appeal. It keeps people from snooping around."

"Although, it is kind of amusing to think about you watching horror movies," Wilder teases, as he lowers his arm from my shoulders.

"I watch them," I insist. "Or, well, I've watched a couple. I had to cover my eyes during the gory parts, though."

"Of course you did." Wilder lightly pulls on a strand of my hair, something he seems to do a lot. Then he walks toward the front porch of the cabin where Xavier and Benton are waiting.

I move to follow him, but Jackson captures the sleeve of my shirt and pulls me back.

"Zhara," he says, caution and worry filling his eyes. "Please, please just remember that, no matter what, things will get better."

I swallow hard, a sense of impending dread flooding through me. Again, I have the compulsion to run, leave the forest, go home, and pretend the last handful of days never happened. But the thing I'm learning is that pretending doesn't erase what's really going on. That I can pretend all I want that the truth doesn't exist, but in the end, it does.

That the truth will always catch up to you.

FOUR
A TUNNEL OF LIES

THE INSIDE of the cabin is exactly what I expected—cobwebs everywhere, a dusty wood stove, no rooms, just open space. A wooden table is in the far back corner of the area, along with a sink. The only other pieces of furniture are a rocking chair and a rug. None of the other guys are here either, leaving me to wonder where they went.

I'm about to ask when Benton crouches down in front of the rug. "We're positive no one followed us, right?" he asks no one in particular.

Xavier retrieves his phone from his pocket, glances at the screen, and then nods. "Ridge says we're good."

So many questions flood my thoughts, ranging from why it matters to how Ridge knows we weren't being followed since he's not here. But, with all the high-tech gear I've seen the guys use, I guess I shouldn't be too surprised, so I keep my questions to myself.

Jackson must note the confusion on my face, though, because he says, "We have to be extra careful that no one knows this place exists. If the wrong person found it and discovered what we were keeping out here, our entire mission could be compromised."

I nod like I understand but wonder what exactly about this cabin would compromise their mission. It's just an old cabin. What's the big deal?

Then Benton lifts the rug up, revealing a trapdoor in the floorboards, and my eyes widen. *People actually have those?*

Jackson chuckles as he catches sight of my expression. "She's cute when she's confused. Or, well, she's just cute in general, but the confusion definitely adds to the cuteness."

Warmth floods my cheeks, causing his grin to broaden.

"Jackson," Benton warns, giving him a hard look.

Jackson shrugs innocently. "What?"

Benton continues to look at him the same way as he opens the trapdoor.

Jackson heaves a sigh. "Whatever, man. God forbid I give her a compliment."

"That's not what you were doing," Benton says, his gaze softens as he glances at me. "You ready for this?"

No. "Um ... Yes ...?" The indecision in my tone causes him to pause.

"Maybe we should wait to do this," he says with hesitancy. "It doesn't have to be today."

Part of me wants to nod, but I find myself shaking my head. "No, I want to know what's going on."

He presses his lips together. "All right." Then, taking a deep breath, he drops into the trapdoor.

Wilder steps up beside me and gently places his hand on the small of my back. "You go down next. We'll follow right behind you."

Biting my bottom lip, I nervously glance at the three of them. Then I shuffle toward the trapdoor. Nervousness bubbles through me, so much so that my knees wobble a bit. But I keep moving forward, toward the truth. Sitting down on the floor, I lower my feet through the trapdoor.

"So, I just jump?" I ask, glancing at the three of them.

"Hold on." Xavier steps toward the trapdoor and peers down it. "Benton?"

"Yep, I'm right here." Hands touch my legs as his voice floats up from the darkness. "I've got you, Zhara. Just lower yourself down."

It dawns on me then how very horror-movie-like this scene is. Girl goes into the woods with a bunch of guys, girl goes into a cabin with the guys, girl goes into a hole in the floor with the guys.

Am I stupid for trusting them?

Before I can arrive at a conclusion, Benton lightly tugs on my legs, just enough for me to fall forward and into the trapdoor.

I gasp, squeezing my eyes shut, panicking as, for a split-second, I'm not sure where I'm falling to. Then a pair of arms wrap around my waist, and the warm scent of Benton's cologne floods my nostrils.

"I've got you," he says, holding me against his solid chest.

I nod, clutching on to his shoulders. "Thanks."

The warmth of his breath dusts my cheeks as he exhales. "Don't thank me for catching you when it's my fault you had to fall anyway."

I feel like he's speaking in code. A code I don't understand. Then, to add to my seemingly constant confusion, he brushes his lips against my cheek.

My eyes snap open, my gaze colliding with his. He looks at me for a beat with a crease between his brows. Then he sets me down and turns away, walking off as if nothing happened.

And maybe nothing really did. I mean, he's kissed me a handful of times. But those were all part of the job. Well, except for the first time we kissed, which was also my first kiss ...

Man, it seems like forever ago yet, in reality, it was only about a week.

"Come on," Benton says as he starts down the ... dirt path?

What in the crap?

My eyes widen as I take in my surroundings. The kiss had distracted me enough that I hadn't really paid attention. Now that I am ...

I shake my head in astonishment as my gaze skims across the tunnel that burrows into the dirt, stretching far enough that I can't see where it leads. But I can see, thanks to the florescent lights covering the cement ceiling.

"How is this here?" I ask Benton. "I mean, how did you ...? What is this ...?" I can't seem to form words.

"About a couple months after we all joined the program and learned that the agency was going to be part of every aspect of our lives, we decided we needed a place of our own that not even the agency could be a part of," Benton explains, threading his fingers through mine as he leads me down the tunnel. "So, we all chipped in and bought this place under an alias so no one would know we bought it. Most of this already existed. I think the owner was one of those people who was planning for the apocalypse or something." He slows to a stop in front of a door. "But yeah, anyway, Ridge installed a bunch of security so no one but us can get past this area." He lets go of my hand, flips up a lid to a compartment ...

No, not a compartment. A hand scanner, something I realize as he places his palm on the pad inside the compartment. Lights flash then a series of *clicks* fill the air, like doors unlocking, which probably is exactly what it is since the door in front of us glides open.

I gape at him stupidly. "I don't ... How? I know you said Ridge installed this, but it's almost straight out a science fiction novel or something."

Benton shakes his head. "Nah, security like this is actually way more common than you realize. You just probably haven't been to any of the places that have them."

"Okay." I give a short pause. "But how do you guys have stuff like this? I mean, isn't it expensive? And where do you even buy things like this?" Realizing how nosey I'm being, I say, "I'm sorry. None of that is any of my business."

"You don't need to apologize for asking questions," he assures me as he slowly leads me into the room on the other side of the door. "And to answer your questions, we can afford to buy this thanks to Jackson and his massive inheritance. And we have access to this type of equipment because our job lets us make a lot of various and valuable connections."

I nod, my mind stuck on the first thing he said. "Jackson has an inheritance? Does that mean ... someone he knew died?"

Benton nods, giving me a compassionate look. "He lost his parents quite a long time ago."

My lips form an O. Poor Jackson. No wonder he freaks out when people he knows get hurt. And I can relate to that. My heart aches for him, just thinking about it.

As if sensing where my thoughts are, Benton gently squeezes my hand. "He's fine. It was a long time ago."

"Yeah, but ... I don't think anyone really gets over something like that, do they?" I mutter, wishing I had the answer myself.

Benton's sympathy doubles. "Come on; let me show you the rest of the place."

Latching on to the distraction, I let him lead me into the room.

If I thought the tunnel was a shocking sight to behold, boy, oh boy, was I wrong.

"This is ..." I can't even form the words as I turn in a circle, taking in the screens covering the cement walls and the beams covering the ceiling. Like the walls, the floor in the room is made of concrete, and a fancy looking lounge area has been set up along the back area that includes a sofa, a table, a mini fridge ...

"How do you guys even get power down here?" I ask as I take everything in.

"You remember that shed behind the cabin?" Benton asks as he watches me observe everything. When I nod, he says, "Ridge set up a solar power source inside there. It's his own invention."

"Oh." That's all I say. All I can say. I'm too shocked to say anything else.

All of this, the space, the lounge area, it's so crazy it exists down here. But what really surprises me and kind of confuses me are the screens covering the walls. Or, well, not really the screens per se, but what's on them.

Landscapes, towns, neighborhoods. I'm pretty sure the

screens are connected to surveillance cameras, but not all the places are in Honeyton.

"Where are these places?" I wonder as I step toward a wall covered with screens. "And why are you watching them?"

He steps up beside me, his gaze locked on my face. "Some of them are of our homes ... It's our way of keeping an eye on things."

"You mean, your family?" I ask, and he nods. "That's kind of nice, I guess." A little weird, but all of this is weird, so ...

"It's not for nice reasons." He stuffs his hands into his pockets, tension rippling from him. "Most of our families ... what's left of them ... they're not trustworthy. And that's why we need to be careful all the time about what we tell who. I hope you'll do the same, especially with what we're about to tell you."

"I will." I can't help thinking of my own family and if any of them knew that our parents were in the undercover program, running around with drug lords.

Taking me with them when they go see drug lords.

I swallow hard at the painful reminder, but shove the pain down, not wanting to focus on it right now. "So, is this the training pit?"

He shakes his head. "No ... We were going to take you there, but then we realized that, with what we need to tell you ... it might be better if we were someplace more private."

I gulp down a shaky breath. "I guess that makes sense." I grow fidgety, wringing my hands and fiddling with the hem of my shirt. "I'm nervous," I admit, which is completely out of character for me, but anxiety is taking over.

I'm about to start babbling when Wilder and Jackson enter

the room and join Benton and me. I eyeball the door, waiting for Xavier to walk in, but he doesn't.

"Where's Xavier?" Benton asks the same thing I'm thinking.

Wilder and Jackson trade a cautious look before Jackson says, "He went out to get some fresh air. I think he might be struggling a bit with"—his gaze fleeting strays to me before returning to Benton—"this."

Benton smashes his lips together, worry flooding his expression as he nods. "That's fine." He pauses for a moment before blowing out an uneven exhale. "Should we do this?"

At first, I think he's talking to the guys, but then he looks at me.

It's a little weird to be making my own decisions, having spent so much of my life not doing so, but I must be getting used to it because of how easily I'm able to nod.

The guys seem to be struggling a little bit more, all of them hesitating before turning and heading toward the sofa.

Benton laces his fingers through mine, pulling me with him as he crosses the room and plops down on the smaller of the two sofas. Wilder sits down on the longer one, while Jackson heads over to a desk. He collects a laptop then plops down on the sofa beside Wilder. Then he opens up the laptop, rolls up his sleeves, and clicks a few keys. The light of the screen illuminates in his eyes as he continues to click keys and tap the mouse. Then he suddenly just stops.

The room grows quiet then, the three of them just sitting there and trading cryptic looks. They must be having a silent conversation, though, because Jackson finally sighs.

"Fine, I'll do it," he mutters, shaking his head.

"I can do it," Benton says, reaching for the laptop.

Jackson shakes his head and moves the laptop out of Benton's reach. "None of us are going to be able to handle more stuff if you don't let us handle more stuff."

Benton freezes with his arm stretched out. He considers what Jackson said then withdraws his hand, letting out a quiet breath as he reclines on the sofa and crosses his arms. "All right, go ahead then."

Nervousness creeps into Jackson's expression as he sets the laptop on the table between us. His nervousness seems to radiate through the room, as Wilder and Benton both grow squirmy.

"Benton's told you a little bit about the experimental drug facilities, right?" Jackson finally speaks, his blue-eyed gaze fastened on me and crammed with worry.

I anxiously wet my lips with my tongue and nod. "Yeah, he has."

"Good." He actually sounds like he thinks it's the opposite. "Okay, then I won't bore you with explaining it again. I'll just ..." He glances at the screen again. "Shit, this is hard."

He starts shaking his head, muttering curses under his breath and saying nothing that makes much sense. I wait for either Wilder or Benton to take over and explain to me what's going on. But neither of them do.

Finally, I can't take it anymore.

I blame what I do next on stress and lack of sleep, but honestly, I feel like a completely different person as I reach across the table, grab the laptop, and flip it around so I can see what's on the screen.

"Zhara ..." Benton starts, straightening and reaching for the computer.

I smack his hand away. Yes, me, Zhara Baker, actually smacks someone's hand.

But am I even Zhara Baker? Because what's on the screen suggests otherwise.

It appears to be a file about a girl named Mia M. If there wasn't a photo in the upper right-hand corner, I would've thought this was just a file of a random girl. But no, the photo is of me when I was younger.

"Why does this file say my name is Mia M.?" I utter shakily. "Or, is it just mislabeled?"

When none of them make any effort to explain, I glance up. They're all watching me with severe concern and hesitancy. None of them want to tell me the truth, which means the truth is bad.

I glance back at the screen and start skim reading, a chill slowly taking over my body.

"What is this ...? Why does this make it seem like I'm ... like I used to be in a drug facility as a test subject ...? That's not true ... I've spent all my life with my family ... I know that ..." I shake my head, slamming the laptop shut. "I know who I am ... I think I do, anyway ..." My mind races, overflowing with everything that's happened, what I've learned over the last week, the random memories I keep having.

Jackson leans forward and rests his arms on his knees, looking at me. "I know this is a lot to take in; trust me. But Zhara, we're pretty certain this is you. I know the name doesn't match up, but—"

"It isn't true!" I cry out, startling all of us. Never have I yelled that loud before. It sounds unnatural. And I almost apologize. But then I glance at the screen again and something shatters inside me.

"I need to get out of here," I mutter, bolting for the door.

I can't breathe. It feels like the walls are closing in. Like I'm leaving my body and watching someone else. I need some fresh air. Some space to clear my head.

"Zhara!" Benton shouts from behind me. It's followed by the sound of footsteps rushing after me.

I quicken my pace, running out of the room and into the tunnel. I plan on running straight back to the trapdoor, hoping there's a ladder so I can easily get up, but then I slam on the brakes when I round a corner and nearly run into Xavier.

I expect him to ask me what I'm doing, but he doesn't. Instead, he steps to the side and out of my way, like he wants me to leave. And, right now, I'm on the same page as him.

I hurry past him, folding my fingers into fists as my body trembles from the emotional overload I'm feeling right now.

"Don't wander too far," Xavier calls after me, causing me to pause. "It's easy to get turned around, even if you stick to the path. Just get some fresh air, process everything, clear your head, and then come back in. We can keep an eye on you from the cameras, so you'll be safe."

Smashing my lips together, I nod without glancing at him. Then I take off in a mad sprint, running back to where the trapdoor is. There isn't a ladder, but steps have been carved into the wall, so I'm able to easily get out. Then I burst out of the cabin, rush down the stairs, and start running. I make it to the edge of the path before I sink to my knees.

Part of me doesn't want to cry, knowing the guys might be watching me. I hate that they'd see me breaking apart like that. Hate that I'm breaking apart at all. Even at my parents' funeral, I held it together, only crying when I was locked in my room by myself. Crying shows that not everything is okay. And everything is supposed to be okay.

I'm supposed to have it all together. That's who I am.

Aren't I?

I don't know anymore.

Who I am.

Where I came from.

If I'm Zhara Baker.

I don't even know if I ever was her.

And if I wasn't …

… Then it means everything I thought I knew about my life was a lie.

FIVE

LIGHTNING BOLTS AND THE UNKNOWN

I'M NOT certain how long I stay kneeling in the dirt, crying my eyes out. Long enough that clouds roll in and thunder begins booming in the distance. I should get up and move; go inside before the rain starts. But I can't seem to find the will.

I feel so heavy, so broken.

I'm just about to lie down and curl up in a ball, stay there until the rain arrives and hopefully washes me away, when I hear the sound of approaching footsteps. I assume it's one of the guys, probably Benton since he's usually the one who has these kinds of talks with me. So, I'm a bit surprised when a set of Converse sneakers appear in my vision.

I glance up, my teary-eyed gaze meeting Jackson's sympathetic one.

He studies me for a slamming heartbeat of a second before crouching down in front of me. "We wanted to give you a bit of time to yourself, but it's about to rain and ... everyone's starting to get really worried."

"Sorry." I sniffle then lift my hand to wipe my eyes on the sleeve of my shirt. Then I remember I'm wearing Xavier's leather jacket, so I use my fingertips instead.

"Don't apologize," he tells me. "You have every right to cry, especially about something like this. I know I cried when I found out."

"You cried when you found out I might be from an ... experimental drug facility?" Saying the words aloud makes my chest pressurize and tears sting my eyes again. But I suck them back, trying to pull myself together.

He shakes his head, wisps of his blond hair falling into his eyes. "No, when I found out *I* was from one. Although, it did break my heart when I learned about you."

My heart thunders in my chest. "You were from a drug facility, too?"

He gives a small nod. "From the ages of three to six. So, for three years. I don't remember any of it, though. Memory loss is a side effect of some of the drugs that were tested on me."

While I did glance at that file on the laptop, I didn't read every detail, so I'm not sure if ... "I know that file said I was from a drug facility, but does that mean ... does that mean drugs were tested on me?"

He sucks in an unsteady breath. "I want to say there's a chance that maybe they weren't, but then I'd be lying to you."

"No more lies please," I whisper as the weight of reality sets in.

I was a test subject at some drug facility.

Drugs were tested on me.

And when I think about it, it kind of makes sense. The memory loss I experienced, my weird body temperature, how I never get sick.

Tears well in my eyes again. "What does this make me?"

He cups my face between his hands and swipes a few tears from my cheeks. "This doesn't change who you are. You're still Zhara."

"That file says my name was Mia M." I sniffle. "I don't even have a last name."

"Your last name is Baker. Just because you now know about your past, doesn't change who you are. Your parents are still your parents, and your family is still your family, even if they might not be related to you by blood. And you can't let knowing this take that away from you. You can't let the people from these facilities take any more away from you."

I smash my quivering lips together as I nod.

Deep down, I know he's right. But accepting what he's saying means accepting that this is my truth. That I am from a drug facility.

As my breathing quickens, Jackson lowers his hands from my face. "Come on; let's take a walk." He slips his fingers through mine and pulls me to my feet.

I latch on to his hand as I steady myself. Then we silently walk down the path and into the shadows of the trees.

Neither of us speaks, and I'm okay with that. Words hurt right now.

Everything hurts right now.

But it is getting a bit easier to breathe, knowing I'm not completely alone in this.

We walk for quite a while, turning down several different paths, and eventually, rain begins to trickle from the sky. Still, we continue walking, the branches above offering a bit of shelter, but not a lot. The old Zhara would've freaked out about getting her hair wet and her feet getting muddy. This Zhara, though, lets the mud seep into her sandals, lets her hair get wet, lets the coldness set in and erase everything else she's feeling.

Great. I'm talking to myself in the third person. Maybe I'm crazy. Maybe the drugs tested on me made me crazy.

"You know, I was adopted after I was rescued from the drug facility," Jackson suddenly says. "I lived with the family for about two years before they died in a car accident. I was happy, though, during those two years. That I can remember."

I swallow hard as my gaze slides to him. He's staring ahead at the trees, raindrops dripping down his face and from the wet strands of his hair. His shirt is soaked, too, and his sneakers are covered in mud, but he doesn't seem to care. How could he when he's thinking about his dead parents?

It's strange seeing him like this. All through school and for most of the time over the last week, he's always seemed like the sort of guy who didn't have a care in the world. Always flirting and laughing and joking around. I never would've expected him to be carrying this sort of weight on his shoulders. Honestly, I never expected to *be* in a situation like this. Never expected things like this to exist.

"I'm sorry ... That your parents died, I mean," I tell him quietly. "I know how hard that is."

He meets my gaze. "I know you do. That's why I'm telling you this. I don't tell a lot of people, mostly because, unless you've lost a parent, you can't understand the sort of pain that comes with that ... and the worry of losing someone else."

I nod understandingly. "For weeks after my parents died, I couldn't sleep. I was afraid that, if I did, I'd end up losing one of my siblings ... I used to walk around at night and peek in their bedrooms to make sure they were okay." I shake my head at myself. "That probably makes me sound creepy, right?"

He shakes his head. "Not at all. Honestly, if I had siblings when my adoptive parents died, I probably would've done the same thing."

"So, you don't have any siblings?"

"Unfortunately, no. It would've made things easier if I did. Maybe I wouldn't have ended up ..." He trails off, his throat muscles working as he swallows hard.

My brows dip together. "Ended up what?"

He assesses me, his eyelashes fluttering against the rain. "After my adoptive parents died, my aunt ... or, well, my adoptive mother's sister moved into the house to take care of me." He scratches his cheek as he looks away. "Things got really lonely and complicated after that. My ... aunt, she wasn't a huge fan of kids, so she basically didn't want anything to do with me. I spent a lot of years by myself which, whatever, I'm okay with that now. But I've always wondered if things would've been a little bit easier if I'd had a brother or sister to talk to about stuff." He grows quiet, dazing off for a bit. Then he shakes his head and shrugs as he looks at me. "But that's all in the past. Now I have the guys. And while they can annoy the fuck out of me"—the corners of his lips quirk upward—"I'm glad I have them. I also have the program and a purpose. It's easier now."

I bite my bottom lip. "I'm glad you're okay now, but ... how did you find out you were from an experimental drug facility? Did your adoptive parents tell you before they passed away?"

"I wish they had. It probably would've been easier if they had. Unfortunately, the aunt was the one to break the news to me." He pauses briefly, tension rippling through his body. "She did it when she found out my parents left all their money to me. She tried to say that I somehow brainwashed them into doing it, that the drugs that were injected into me made me crazy, like she thought I was some sort of monster."

I swallow the lump wedged in my throat. "That's awful."

"She was kind of an awful person," he says with a shrug. "But it doesn't really matter. She didn't win her case."

I don't say anything.

While he may be pretending everything is okay, I doubt he still isn't affected by what happened. Sure, you don't have to let the past control you, and you can move past stuff, but memories are connected to our emotions, and when we remember them, those emotions can sometimes creep up on us.

"My adoptive parents were actually part of the program," he continues. "So was my aunt."

"Was?"

"Yeah, she retired. Or, well, the program forced her to." He smiles a little at that.

I wipe a few water droplets from my forehead. "Why? What'd she do?"

His smile expands, and he looks like the Jackson I know. "She went crazy after she started doing a bunch of drugs. Ironic, right?"

A trace of a smile touches my lips. "It kind of is."

He grins. "It totally is."

And for a moment, everything doesn't feel so heavy, and a spark of hope flickers through me that maybe, just maybe, everything will turn out okay. Then something dawns on me.

"If I'm from an experimental drug facility, does that mean Alexis isn't my twin? Because we're not identical, and I ..." I force down a lump welling in my throat. "Or, is she from an experimental drug facility, too?" I don't know what answer will hurt the worst.

No, I do. I don't want Alexis to have to feel what I'm feeling right now. But, considering she's currently with another group, I have a feeling that might not be the case.

Jackson comes to a stop. Since he's holding my hand, I have to stop with him. That's okay. My feet are getting really tired.

"Honestly, I'm not sure," he tells me. "There wasn't much in your file. And we couldn't find one on Alexis. But it doesn't mean the answers aren't there. It just means we need to look harder."

I nod, those stupid tears wanting to come out again. "Okay."

Jackson places a hand on my cheek. "It might take some time, but we'll get you some answers." He pauses then the corners of his lips quirk upward. "Cute girl."

Strands of my damp hair stick to my face as I shake my head. His use of the nickname he gave me almost makes things feel normal.

For a moment, anyway.

As lightning flashes brightly, illuminating our surroundings, Jackson glances up at the sky. "Shit, the storm's getting really bad." Raindrops splatter onto his forehead as he looks back at me. "I don't want to force you to go inside until you're ready, but I'm also a bit worried we might get our asses zapped if we stand out here for too much longer."

He has a good point, but that doesn't make it any easier to say I'm ready.

Ready to return to the guy's secret hideout.

Ready to see the looks on their faces.

Ready to move forward and accept the truth of my past.

But, as another bolt of lightning zaps across the sky and thunder echoes it, I decide it's time.

Time to face my future.

Whatever that may be.

SIX

PRETTY NEW SHOES

BY THE TIME Jackson and I arrive back at the cabin, the sky is covered with dark clouds that occasionally light up with a lightning bolt. Rain is pouring down, soaking the land, our clothes, and our hair. And our shoes?

Yeah, what shoes?

"I can't even see my feet anymore?" I remark as we hike through the mud toward the collapsed front porch.

I'm trying really hard not to think about what I may be, how I could be Mia M., how my life might be one big lie.

Jackson pauses, glancing down at my feet. Then he chuckles. "At least we match." He lifts up his own foot, revealing that nearly every inch of his sneakers is covered in mud. Then he taps his foot against mine. "We can be muddy feet buddies."

I snort a laugh, and then my eyes widen, the sound surprising me.

I didn't think I could laugh after everything I just learned.

Jackson seems a bit surprised, too, but then a smile

stretches across his lips. "Aw, I got you to laugh. I think that makes me, like, the best muddy feet buddy ever."

I shake my head, unable to keep a smile from pulling at my lips.

It's nice. To smile and laugh.

And it gives me a bit of hope that maybe I'll be able to get past this one day.

Of course, I think, before that happens, I'll have to get some answers. I just hope Jackson meant what he said. That the guys will help me get those—

I slam to a halt when my foot sinks so far down into the mud that I can't get it out.

"Crap ... I'm stuck." I wiggle my foot, trying to get unstuck, but I swear I keep sinking deeper.

And then, to add to the situation, my other foot becomes stuck.

I frown as I bend down and try to dig my way out, but that only leads to my hands and arms getting covered with mud.

Jackson watches me for a raindrop of a second with an amused smile on his face. "I'm sorry, but this is literally the most amusing thing I've seen all day."

I grimace, sweeping my wet hair out of my face. "I think I'm stuck."

He bites back a laugh. "Really? I couldn't tell."

I sigh, jutting my lip out. "I sometimes think I'm the most klutzy person in the world. When I was little, I'd trip over everything. Even things that weren't there. It got a bit better as I got older, but this"—I gesture at my feet—"clearly proves I was wrong."

He grins. "Maybe. But at least you look cute all covered in mud."

Warmth spreads across my cheeks, but I doubt he can see it with how dark it's gotten.

"You look so cute that I'm deciding if maybe I should just leave you here for a while," he teases. "I'll come back to get you in a while when you're good and muddy." His eyes light up with playfulness. "And then we can have a mud wrestling match." He winks at me. "Don't worry; I'll go easy on you. And we can totally keep some of our clothes on."

My cheeks grow even warmer, my eyes widening. "What? Why would we take off any of our clothes?"

"Because you have to get naked to mud wrestle," he says with hilarity in his tone, sounding like his joking self again.

My heart rate quickens, and my face heats even more. "I don't ... I can't ..." Oh my gosh, I sound like a babbling idiot. So you know, sounding like my normal self again.

A beat of silence stretches between us, raindrops splattering all around us. Then Jackson suddenly busts up laughing.

"I'm just messing with you, cute girl." He gives a short pause then steps toward me. "I'd never leave you out here in the rain like that." He crouches down and wraps his hand around my ankle, smiling to himself. "Although, I'd definitely like to mud wrestle with you someday. Preferably naked."

Oh my God! My cheeks are on fire.

I stand there stupidly, unsure of what to say.

He chuckles again, muttering something about me being "so damn cute." Then he pulls my foot out of the mud. Unfortunately, my shoe doesn't come with it.

"Hold on," he says. "Let me get your other foot out, and then I'll dig your shoes out." He moves his hand to my other ankle and tugs that foot out pretty easily, but that shoe gets lost in the mud, too.

Once I'm free from the evil mud's grasp, I crouch down beside him, and we use our hands to search for my sandals. But the ground has become too much of a mess and is only getting worse as the rain continues to shower down. In fact, it's getting so bad that a small stream has formed in front of us, sweeping some of the land away.

Finally, Jackson removes his hands from the mud and looks at me. "Do you have any personal attachment to those shoes?"

I shake my head. "Not really. But they're the only ones I have with me now."

"I'll just get you a pretty new pair," he tells me, standing and wiping his hands on the sides of his pants, which doesn't really do any good since his pants are covered in mud, too.

"You don't need to buy me a new pair," I insist, standing up. "I can just go home and grab some more. When I can go home anyway ... No one ever said when I could?"

"I'm sure we can find a way to let you go back to your house, at least long enough to grab some clothes. Or, at least one of us can do that for you. It might be better for one of us to do it. At least until we figure out why your potential rogue of a neighbor was setting off a scanner."

I nod and move to head back to the cabin, his words reminding me of everything going on. I make it only a few steps, though, before he moves around in front of me.

Then he squats down in front of me. "Hop on. I'll give you a piggyback ride back to the cabin."

"I'm okay," I insist. "It's not that far away."

"Yeah, but you don't have any shoes on, and that porch is a sliver death trap."

I eyeball the porch. He has a point. So, taking a deep breath, I climb onto his back.

Once I get situated, he straightens and starts up the muddy path toward the front porch.

"And FYI," he says as he trots up the stairs. "I'm still buying you a pair of shoes."

"Jackson, I swear, it's fine," I say with my arms wrapped around him. "Really. It's not a big deal. And besides, my shoes might turn up after it stops raining."

"Yeah, so what? We're friends now. And friends let friends buy them shoes if they want to." Holding me with one arm, he pulls open the cabin door.

I can't help smiling just a little bit. "We're friends?" I say aloud then instantly want to retract my statement.

I sound like a little kid.

He chuckles. "Of course we are, cute girl. I don't go around offering to buy random people shoes. I only do that for my friends."

His words make me feel all warm inside, but not in an embarrassing sort of way.

"Okay, but you really don't have to buy me shoes."

"But I'm going to when we go shopping here in just a few hours."

Shopping? "Wait. What?"

Before he can answer, we enter the cabin and find Benton waiting for us in the entryway.

His gaze skates over us and a crease forms between his brows. I wonder why. Because I'm on Jackson's back? Wait. I am supposed to be pretending to be his girlfriend. Maybe this is crossing a line. Perhaps I should get down. But I don't want to be rude to Jackson. Will he think it's rude?

I roll my eyes at myself. What is my problem? After everything, this is what I'm worried about?

"We have a problem," Benton announces, crossing the room toward us with his hands stuffed in his pockets.

I feel Jackson's arms stiffen around me as he kicks the door shut behind us.

"By the look on your face, I'm guessing it's really bad," he says.

Benton nods, his gaze flicking from me then back to Jackson. "We were tracked here by Zhara's neighbor."

Fear courses through me. "Creepy Charles?"

"Is that his name?" Benton asks with an arch of his brow.

"Yeah … Well, that's what he told me his name was," I explain. "Is he …? Is he here, looking for me?"

Benton nods then wavers. "Well, he was. We captured him and locked him up. Right now, Xavier is working on getting some answers out of him."

I want to ask him what that means—how Xavier is getting some answers out of him—but the last time I wanted answers, I found out I might be a test subject from a drug facility, so …

Yeah, I think I'm going to keep my questions to myself for now.

SEVEN
FLIRTATIOUS OVERLOAD

AFTER BENTON TELLS us they caught Creepy Charles, he gives a quick recap of how it happened. Apparently, while Jackson and I were outside, Wilder and Benton spotted someone creeping around near the cabin on their security cameras, which are all over the forest. Since it was raining, they were able to sneak out and capture him. Luckily, that was before Creepy Charles found me and Jackson because, apparently, he had a weapon, although Benton is relatively vague on what kind. I think that was on purpose, so he won't frighten me. At this point, I don't think it would've made that big of a difference. Although, that revelation frightens me a bit.

What does that say about what kind of person I am? What kind of person am I even? Who was I in the past? Who am I now? Who will I become? If I was an experimental subject, will the side effects of the drugs eventually change me? Have they already changed me?

"Zhara?" Jackson crouches down in front of me so he can

meet my gaze. "Are you in there?" He smiles, but a hint of concern fills his eyes.

I blink myself from my thoughts and glance around. I'm back in the room with all the screens, sitting on the sofa with a glass of water in my hand and I've taken off Xavier Jacket so it can air dry. The scary part is I can barely remember going through the trapdoor. After that, I'd been so distracted by my thoughts that I just sort of zoned out.

"What's wrong?" I ask Jackson, picking a chunk of mud off my shorts. Not that it does any good. The entire half of my lower body is covered in dried mud that's stuck to my skin. I need to shower. And change my clothes. And get some shoes.

"Nothing's wrong." Jackson takes the glass of water from my hand, sets it down on the table behind him, and then rests his arms on my legs. "I think we should go shopping now."

I blink at him. "Right now? But, what about Creepy Charles?"

He dismisses me with a wave of his hand. "Creepy Charles is detained, and he's not going anywhere for a while."

"But, aren't we waiting to get answers from him?"

"That might take a while, too, and we really don't need to be here for that. Xavier, Benton, Ridge, and Jett can handle that."

I guess he has a point. Although, he did leave one person off his list.

"What about Wilder?"

"Wilder isn't going to miss a chance to go shopping." Wilder appears in the doorway with a grin on his face.

"Wilder is also very creepy by talking about himself in the third person," Jackson remarks, tossing Wilder a smirk from over his shoulder.

Wilder rolls his eyes as he strolls into the room. "Whatever, man. At least I don't refer to myself as ..." He tilts his head to the side. "What was that nickname you gave yourself?" He taps his finger against his pierced lip. "The ladies' man? Or was it sexy hottie?" A sly grin spreads across his face. "No, it was both, wasn't it?"

Jackson shrugs. "Yeah. So what? Both are true." He grins at me. "Right, cute girl? Which, FYI, is a beautiful nickname," he throws over his shoulder at Wilder. "Unlike pink cheeks."

"Hey, I stopped calling her that," Wilder protests, coming to a stop in front of us. "I'm just going with princess for now."

I expect Jackson to give him crap about that, but all he does is nod say, "A much better choice."

"For sure." Wilder winks at me.

So does Jackson.

I start to feel a bit overwhelmed, and I'm not even positive why. Or maybe it's just everything starting to pile up on me.

"So, I'm supposed to go shopping with both of you?" I ask, attempting to distract myself from being overwhelmed.

The two of them trade a sly look then Jackson grins at me. "What? Doesn't that sound fun?"

"Um ... Yeah?" I say as more of a question. Not that I think spending time with them is terrible. It's just that, out of all the guys, these two are the most joking and flirty, and both traits seem to make me blush a lot. I have a feeling if I spend time with both of them together, I might end up starting on fire from embarrassment. Plus, after everything I discovered, should I really be out shopping?

"Come on. Go shopping with us," Jackson says enticingly while brushing a strand of my damp hair out of my face. "It'll take your mind off things."

"Plus, you need to get an outfit for the masquerade party," Wilder adds, plopping down on the sofa beside me and propping his feet onto the coffee table in front of us. "And trust me, out of all of us, Jackson and I have the best taste in clothes, so you're gonna look fucking hot." When I pull a face, he adds, "Or sexy. Or cute. Or lovely. Whatever style you're going for, we'll figure it out."

"It'll be fun," Jackson agrees, smiling at me.

With both of them smiling at me like this, it makes me feel a little lightheaded. Maybe that's why I find myself nodding.

Or maybe I'm just looking for an escape from reality.

EIGHT

SWEET KISSES

BEFORE WE GO SHOPPING, we all decide that Jackson and I need to clean up. And the best way to do that is to go to Jackson and Wilder's house because, apparently, they have their own house, something I didn't know and a reminder that I barely know them. Well, after our talk in the forest, I feel like I know Jackson a bit better.

"Maybe I should go home and shower?" I suggest as we head out of the cabin.

The area is flooded, but thankfully, the sky is clear now, so we're no longer getting rained on.

"You should let me give you another piggyback ride," Jackson offers as we step off the front porch.

"I'm fine," I tell him as I step off the last stair and into the mud.

He glances warily at my bare feet. "You don't have any shoes on, and there are rocks everywhere."

I eye the muddy and rocky path that leads back to where Benton's car is parked. Maybe he has a point.

"Let me give her one," Wilder states as he hops off the last stair and into the mud beside me.

Jackson looks at him with his brow lifted. "Why?"

Wilder shrugs. "You got your turn. Now I want mine."

"Wait ... How did you know he already gave me one?" I ask Wilder with confusion.

Smiling, Wilder points at a camera on the roof of the cabin. "We saw you on those."

I frown, suddenly becoming aware that all the guys probably saw me have my meltdown. Saw me breaking apart. Saw my imperfections.

The frown fizzles from Wilder's face. "Hey, it's okay. We weren't spying on you or anything. We just checked on you a few times to make sure everything was okay."

I can't tell if he's lying or not but decide to move past it. "It's fine."

"Stop using the word fine." He wags a finger at me, playfully scolding me.

A tiny smile touches my lips, which makes him smile.

Then he spins around and squats down in front of me. "Hop on."

For some reason, I glance at Jackson.

He offers me a smile. "You better hop, or else I'm going to." When I laugh softly, he steps toward Wilder. "You think I'm joking?" He moves to hop onto Wilder's back.

"Dude, princess, please just get on my back, so I don't have to give his big butt a piggyback ride to the car," Wilder says in a playful tone.

"Hey, I prefer the term juicy ass," Jackson quips with a grin.

Laughter slips from my lips, and Jackson's grin grows.

"And that is the sound of success," he states, sticking his fist out toward Wilder.

"For sure," Wilder agrees, giving Jackson a fist bump.

I'm a bit puzzled over what they think they were successful at but smile anyway. Then I step forward and carefully climb onto Wilder's back. Then I frown. "I'm getting mud all over you. Maybe I should get down."

Shaking his head, Wilder stands up. "I'll just change when we get to our place." Then he starts forward down the muddy path and Jackson follows.

As we walk, Wilder does his best not to get muddy, but Jackson is covered in mud, so he isn't very cautious, splashing through puddles and soaking the bottom of his pants even more.

"I'm totally going to have to throw these pants away," he remarks as he splashes in another puddle.

"You're so wasteful," Wilder teases then kicks some puddle water on him.

"Dude, don't start something you can't finish," Jackson warns with a dark look.

Wilder just snorts a laugh. "Like you'd splash me while Zhara is on my back."

Jackson's gaze slides to me and a look of deliberation forms on his face. Then a wicked grin curls at his lips. "Well, she's already muddy anyway." Then he kicks puddle water all over Wilder, but he does it low enough that none gets on me. Not that I'd care.

Wilder shakes his head, the bottom of his pants covered in droplets of muddy puddle water. "You just lost points, man."

"Points for what?" Jackson asks, stuffing his hands in his pockets.

"I don't know." Wilder adjusts my weight. "Just points."

They grow quiet, trading a look. I can't see Wilder's face, but Jackson looks contemplative. Then his gaze fleeting flits to me before he looks ahead again.

"How are we going to get Zhara some clean clothes before we go shopping?" Jackson changes the subject, leaving me to wonder what that bizarre exchange was about.

"We could stop by my house?" I suggest again, gripping onto Wilder as he jumps over a puddle. "I mean, if Creepy Charles is here, it should be okay, right?"

Jackson and Wilder trade another look, then Jackson looks at me. "I think, for now, it might be best if you don't go home," he tells me cautiously. "Not until we can figure out why Creepy Charles was staking you out and using a scanner on you."

"Oh." I rub my lips together. "Do you think it has to do with me maybe being a test subject?"

"I'm not sure." He offers me an apologetic look. I'm not sure why, though. None of this is his fault. In fact, all he's done is make me feel a little bit better. "I mean, there's a lot of reasons why, but what we do know is that he's got the rogue mark, so whatever the reason was—"

"Isn't good," Wilder finishes for him as we step out of the trees and onto the open space where Benton's car is parked.

Another car is there, as well, a sleek, dark blue one with tinted windows.

I immediately tense, thinking it's Axel, since his car looks similar.

Wilder must sense my tension because he lightly massages the side of my leg as he says, "Relax. It's just Jackson's driver."

My gaze darts to Jackson. "You have your own driver?"

He gives me an innocent look. "What? Is that not normal?"

"And he's so humble about it," Wilder remarks, his boots shuffling against the damp dirt as he makes his way toward the car.

"Hey, there's nothing wrong with me being proud of the stuff I have," Jackson retorts, removing his hands from his pocket to roll up the sleeves of his shirt.

"I never said there was." Wilder stops beside the back door to the car. "I was just stating a point."

"A very valid one." Jackson slows to a halt beside us, opens the door, and then gestures for us to get inside.

I move to climb off Wilder's back, but he grips on to me and turns around so his back is facing the open door. Then he crouches down and levels me with the seat so I can slide right in without my feet having to touch the ground.

"Look, he does know how to be a gentleman," Jackson mocks, glancing at his phone.

"Yeah, you should take notes," Wilder retorts, straightening and stretching his arms above his head. "So, how long do we have before we need to be ready for tonight?"

Jackson nods at the car. "Climb in. We can talk on the way."

Wilder salutes him then climbs into the back seat.

I start to slide over to give him room, but he moves around me and sits down on my other side so, when Jackson climbs in, I'm wedged between the two of them. The scent of rain and mud instantly clings to the air after Jackson shuts the door.

A tinted window is separating the front seat from the back seat, but when Jackson pushes a button, it rolls down. On the other side is an older woman with grey hair pulled into a bun.

"Hey, May," he greets her with a charming grin.

"Hey, sweetie," she greets back, grinning at him in the rearview mirror.

"Dude, May"—he laughs, sinking back in the seat—"please don't call me that in front of this lovely girl." He gives a not-so-discreet nod toward me.

May chuckles. "All right, *sir*." She rolls her eyes. "Where to?"

"Home," Jackson says, kicking off his shoes.

She nods then backs up the car.

"Thank you, May," Jackson tells her then rolls up the window.

Wilder immediately laughs. "I can't believe she still calls you that."

"Hey, don't dis my nickname," Jackson protests with a grin. "I like it."

"Okay." A mischievous twinkle sparkles in Wilder's eyes. "I guess I'll start calling you it then."

"Only behind closed doors," Jackson warns, pointing a finger at him.

"Okay, sweetie." Wilder flashes him a grin.

Jackson throws one right back at him. Then he reclines back in the seat and drapes his arm across the back of it, the crook of his elbow resting right behind my head.

"So, what exactly did we decide about the clothes situation?" Wilder leans back and gets comfortable, too, his knee resting against mine, and so is his shoulder.

Being wedged between the two of them makes my heart rate increase, my pulse pounding, and my skin warms. I'm not even sure why I'm reacting this way, other than they're both touching me. Not that it means anything. I'm just not used to it.

Gosh, I'm so stinking awkward sometimes. Seriously, who gets so nervous about sitting between two guys? And now, of all times. With everything that's happened this seems like it should be the last thing on my mind.

On a positive note, though, at least I'm not blushing.

"We could always just have her go naked," Jackson says with a sly grin.

So much for not blushing.

I aim a dirty look at him, my cheeks fiery red, I'm sure. "No way."

"Look at you. Trying to be all tough." Jackson brushes his knuckles across my cheek. "The blush, though, it just makes you too damn adorable."

I shake my head, wishing I had a rock to crawl under.

"I've honestly never seen a girl blush so much," Wilder remarks, rotating in the seat so his knee is resting against the side of my leg. "It's why I called her pink cheeks."

"Blush or not, you never should call her that again," Jackson stresses. "Yeah, she's cute when she blushes, but that just means she needs a cute nickname."

"I already changed it to princess," Wilder clarifies, digging his phone out from his pocket.

Jackson crinkles his nose. "That doesn't seem very fitting to me."

"You should see her room," Wilder says distractedly as he reads a text. "It's all pink and glitter and fluffiness."

"Hey, it's not that bad," I protest then sigh. "Okay, actually it is."

"You don't need to be embarrassed about your room," Jackson tells me. "Own who you are."

"That's the thing, though," I mutter. "I'm not even sure who I am."

Jackson's expression softens. "Don't let what you found out today make you question who you are."

"I'm not questioning it," I insist. "I just ..." I shrug.

Wilder pockets his phone then gives me his undivided attention. "You just what?"

I shrug again, picking at my fingernails, not sure if I want to talk to these guys about how, for years, I've felt like I'm not sure who I am, but I'm definitely not the perfect Zhara that I pretended to be. I mean, sure, I've talked to Benton a little bit about it, but only because we got locked in the bathroom together and I tend to babble while I'm nervous. But I never told him all the details, like how I feel like I don't know who I am.

"If you don't want to talk about it, you don't have to," Jackson finally says. "But Wilder and I are excellent listeners."

"And we won't hate you if you admit you hate pink," Wilder says, his lips quirking with amusement. "Or, if you like it, we're totally cool with that, too."

"Pink can be fun," Jackson adds, raking his fingers through his hair and making the strands go askew. "I own some pink shirts and shoes."

"I have a pair of pink boxers," Wilder informs me then reaches for the waistband of his pants. "In fact, I might have them on right now." He tugs down the waistband enough to see the top of his boxers, and in the process, the hem of his shirt slips up.

I try not to stare, but I can't seem to help it. My gaze strays to his abs. And not because he's ripped or anything like that. Well, he's in shape for sure, his muscles toned and lean, but his flesh is also covered in scars. Long, thin scars, as if some animal clawed him.

"What happened?" I whisper.

When Wilder stiffens, tugging down his shirt and covering up the scars, I realize I said the wrong thing.

"I'm sorry. You don't need to answer that." I tear my attention off him and focus on the space in front of me.

"You're fine," Wilder mumbles from beside me. "I didn't mean for you to see those, but I get why you'd ask. They're pretty fucking hideous."

I shake my head, looking at him. "There're not hideous. They're just ..." I search for the right word, but all I can come up with is, "heartbreaking."

His brows furrow. "Heartbreaking?"

"Sorry. That's a really strange word choice. I just meant that whatever caused them had to be painful and hurt. And that's sad that you had to go through something like that." Great, now I'm rambling.

No wonder I don't have any real friends. Well, besides Jackson. But perhaps after hearing me ramble like an idiot, he'll take back the offer.

Wilder stares at me with a pucker at his brow, his lips parting then shutting. Appearing beyond bewildered, he fixes his shirt. "It's fine. It really is."

He sinks into silence then, crossing his arms and staring out the window.

I'm not sure what to say or do, if he's upset with me or what. And again, I'm reminded of why I don't have any real friends.

"Hey, why don't we figure out what you're going to tell

your family?" Jackson interrupts my worrying thoughts, lightly massaging my shoulder.

I turn to look at him, and he offers me a reassuring smile. "About what?"

He brushes his fingers along my shoulder. "About why you're not going to be home for a bit."

"Right. That's a good idea." I pick at a flake of mud on my shirt. "I'm not sure what to say. I'm almost always home, except for when I am—was—at school."

"Could you tell them you're staying at Taylor's?" Jackson suggests, playing with my hair.

Taylor was—is—my friend, but she rarely opens up to me. And at Benton's party, she basically admitted that she feels like we don't have anything in common.

And I'm unsure why he seems so content with touching me. I'm sure I smell, and my hair is wet, yet he continues to ravel a strand of my hair around his finger. All my thoughts center on the way it feels, the way a light shiver rolls through my body. I probably shouldn't be thinking about it. It doesn't mean anything. I should be focusing on what I'm going to tell Loki.

Focus, Zhara, focus.

Come up with something.

A lie.

The problem is I suck at lying.

"I wonder what Alexis told Loki," I say aloud. "I bet she came up with something good."

Jackson's eyes light up then. "You should text her and see. If she hasn't told him anything, maybe you could both tell him you're going on a trip together, like to celebrate your graduation."

"That could work, I guess." But I'm still hesitant. "The problem is Alexis and I aren't very close anymore."

"Well, this fake trip could be a chance for you guys to grow close," Jackson says with a pressing look.

I nod. "You know what? That might work." That doesn't make me feel any better, though, as I take out my phone. "Where should we go?"

Jackson thrums his finger against his lips. "Hmm ... Paris is nice. London, too. I've always wanted to go to Scotland."

"We can't go out of the country," I inform him, although I don't think he's very serious. "I don't even have a passport."

His brows rise. "You don't have a passport?"

I shake my head. "I've never had a reason to get one. I've never had the opportunity to go overseas. My sister Jessamine is actually in London, though."

A calculating look crosses Jackson's face. "One day, I think I'm going to take you out of the country."

He says it like we'll be friends for a long time.

Is that possible?

Will our friendship last beyond this whole undercover thing?

"Where will we go?" I ask, hoping I don't sound too eager.

Jackson's baby blues sparkle with delight as he combs his fingers through my hair. "Where do you want to go?"

I give a half-shrug. "I've honestly never thought about it."

He playfully tugs on a strand of my hair. "Well, think about it now."

I do as he says and think about a place I've always wanted to go. The problem is I've spent most of my life thinking about one thing: going to college and making my parents proud of me. I've never thought of what I'd do if I got the chance to travel.

"How about Scotland, since you've never been there?" I suggest.

His brow arches. "That's where you want to go?" When I nod, he grins. "Then I guess Scotland it is."

"Do I get to go?" Wilder says abruptly from beside me.

When I glance at him, he's smiling at me.

I mentally let out a breath of relief, glad he's no longer upset. "If you want."

He rests his shoulder against mine and leans against me. "I want." Then he threads his fingers through mine, a move Jackson seems to notice and appears a bit puzzled by but doesn't comment on.

The move confuses me, too, but, like Jackson, I don't comment on it, because I'm not really sure what to say. All the guys have been touching me, holding my hand, playing with my hair, and I'm starting to think it's just part of the job.

Yeah, that's probably what it is.

"Why don't you text Alexis and see if she's told Loki anything yet," Jackson suggests, his brow crinkling as his own phone goes off inside his pocket.

Nodding, I send Alexis a text message, asking if she's told Loki anything and, if not, does she think the trip idea is a good one.

She responds within seconds.

Alexis: I'm glad you came up with an idea, because I honestly had no fucking clue what to tell him. The trip thing might work.

Me: Okay. Any idea of where we should say we're going?

Alexis: Just tell him we're going on a road trip. That way, we can be vague.

Me: What about going home, though? Won't it be weird if we just take off?

Alexis: We'll probably have to go home for a bit. I'll have to talk to the guys and figure out a way. For right now, I'm just going to tell Loki I'm spending the night at a friend's. And then maybe tomorrow we can somehow find a way to go home and pack up some stuff.

I have so many questions I want to ask her, so many things I want to tell her, but Benton told me that I need to be careful about what I say via text.

Me: Okay, text me when you know.

Alexis: Okay.

My shoulders feel sort of heavy as I put my phone away. I think all the secrecy might be getting to me, but I don't know what to do about it, or if there's anything I can do.

"Is she okay with the plan?" Wilder says, startling me.

I nod. "Yeah. But she made a point, we'll still have to go home for a bit so we can pack our stuff and pretend to leave. She can't do it today, so she's going to tell Loki she's staying the night at a friend's place, which I guess I should, too."

Wilder searches my eyes. "Why do you seem so sad about that?"

I shrug. "I just hate having to lie."

The corners of Wilder's lips tug upward. "Has anyone ever told you that you have a good soul?"

I shake my head. "Is that a good thing?"

"It's an incredibly good thing. Maybe one day you'll let me paint a portrait of you. Let me see if I can capture that good soul on a canvas." He stares at me expectantly, waiting for me to answer.

I chew on my bottom lip. "I guess, if you want to."

"I want to." He brings my hand to his lips, places a kiss there on my mud-coated skin, and then reclines back in the seat as if nothing happened.

Me? My heart is going crazy inside my chest. I'm not even sure why. It was just a kiss on the hand. A sweet, innocent kiss, yet it has me feeling flustered.

Always flustered.

Why can't I be cool about stuff?

Before I can start delving into that mess of a question, the car slows to a stop.

When I glance up, confusion swirls inside me.

"What is this place?" I ask as I stare at the three-story house that stretches toward the sky. It's so far out in the hills that I've never noticed it before, which makes me realize just how sheltered I have been.

"This is my house." Jackson grins at me as the gates swing open, giving me a better view of the column entrance, the five-car garage, and the acres that stretch for miles and are lined with green grass, blooming flowers, and flourishing trees.

"This is *your house?*" I gape at Jackson.

"Yep, this is my place." He seems amused by my expression. "Well, mine and Wilder's."

"Technically, it's just Jackson's," Wilder chimes in, letting go of my hand so he can stretch and yawn. "He just lets me crash here with him."

I want to ask him why he doesn't have a place of his own, but since he just got over the last personal question I asked him, I decide to take a break from prying into his past.

"How did you get it?" I ask Jackson.

"I got it the same way everyone gets a house." He grins. "I bought it, silly."

I feel stupid. "Sorry. I just wondered how you were able to get such a huge house, but never mind. It doesn't really matter."

"You don't need to apologize," he tells me. "It probably is a bit weird that I'm eighteen and own my own house. And honestly, I didn't really want to own a house yet, but the guys needed a place to hang out when we weren't working under-cover, so I used some of my inheritance money to buy this place. Although the deed has my alias, so no one knows I own it."

"Oh." I eye the gorgeous house. "It's really pretty."

"You're really pretty," he says, and Wilder lets out a sharp cough. Jackson rolls his eyes, his lips parting, but then he frowns as his phone buzzes again. He glances at the screen and worry floods his eyes.

"What's wrong?" I ask, my anxiety spiking.

He promptly shakes his head as he stuffs his phone into his pocket. "It's nothing." But the look he trades with Wilder lets me know that it is something.

Not that I'm going to demand the truth. Maybe it's none of my business anyway. I can't keep a frown from pulling at my lips, though.

Jackson sighs. "Look, I don't want to lie to you, but I also don't want to worry you unless I have to. So, can you just trust me on this and let me keep this to myself until I know for sure if it's worth even worrying you about?"

Pressing my lips together, I nod. "Okay."

"Yeah?" A drop of surprise flickers in his eyes.

I nod again, puzzlement webbing through me. "Yeah. Why are you so surprised?"

He gives a half-shrug. "Trust is a huge deal to me." He pauses then softly kisses me on the cheek. "Thanks for trusting me." The car rolls to a stop then, and he opens the door, jumping out before I can say anything.

Wilder clears his throat loudly again, and I turn to see what's wrong, but he hurriedly climbs out of the car, too.

So weird.

Guys are so weird.

Or maybe I'm just confused, and this is how guys always are?

I shake my head at myself. *Always clueless, Zhara.* Will I ever change?

I'm not sure.

I'm not really sure about anything.

Yep, always Clueless Zhara, I think to myself as I climb out of the car.

Or should I start calling myself Clueless Mia M.?

NINE

JACKSON

I'M TRYING to keep it together as I walk into my house, but I'm really struggling.

The text Benton sent me has my mind racing a million miles a minute. So, the moment we get inside, I tell Wilder to show Zhara to one of the guest bathrooms so she can shower while I go call Benton and get more details as to what the hell is going on.

As they start to head toward the stairway, Zhara suddenly pauses, the awe that's been in her eyes since she saw my house slightly dimming.

"Wait. I don't have anything to change into." She crinkles her nose as she stares at her muddy clothes.

The girl may be covered in mud, but she's still gorgeous. The crazy part is she doesn't even realize it. But that's kind of what makes her *her*. Zhara's always sort of been that girl, the untouchable one who was too good for everyone, too good for any of us. Not because she thinks she's better than everyone, despite the rumors going around school. Honestly, I think it's the opposite. That Zhara doesn't believe she's good enough for anyone. That's something I can relate to.

My aunt liked telling me what a piece of shit I was. I used to believe her until I got older and realized she hated me because of where I came from. That she feared the unknown. Hated it. But that didn't mean I had to hate myself.

After I joined the program, I started to heal a bit. But those old mental scars, the pain connected to them, still gets to me sometimes. And I saw the same pain in Zhara's eyes when she found out about her past. It's why I went out to check on her because, out of all of us, I could relate.

I just wish I could take her pain away.

It's weird, feeling like this. I've spent years flirting and messing around, and now I suddenly feel connected to someone. It's ... strange, to say the least. And I'm not sure what to do with it. Zhara is supposed to be dating Benton, and though the relationship is pretend, I've seen the way Benton looks at Zhara sometimes, that makes me question if he wishes it was for real.

And then there is the whole thing with Wilder kissing her hand and asking if he can paint her. He's almost as big of a flirt as me, but that was more than just flirting.

"Earth to Jacks." Wilder waves his hand in front of my face, drawing me out of my thoughts.

I blink then shake my head at myself. *Get your head in the game, man.* "What's up?"

Wilder gives me a funny look while Zhara stands beside him, looking worried.

"We were trying to figure out what to do about the clothes situation," Wilder says, folding his arms.

My gaze skates across Zhara, and I force a smile onto my

face, force myself to be the flirty Jackson everyone knows. "She could always just go naked. Personally, I like that idea." I grin as Zhara blushes.

God, her blush is so adorable.

Had I made that joke in front of Benton, he would've chewed my ass out. But Wilder just grins.

"Sounds like fun to me," he says.

Zhara's cheeks go bright-ass red. "I can't ... I don't think ..." She stammers for words, totally embarrassed.

And while her stammering is cute as hell, I decide to let her off the hook.

"Oh, fine." I give a dramatic sigh. "I guess you can borrow one of my shirts while we wash your clothes." Okay, that idea doesn't sound too bad. I like the idea of seeing her in my shirt. "Does that sound okay?"

She chews on her bottom lip as she nods. "Yeah, I guess that would work."

"Okay." I offer her a smile before we part ways, Wilder leading her up the stairs while I duck into the office. Then I shut the doors behind me and dial Benton's number.

"Tell me you made it to your house," he answers after one ring, his voice crammed with tension.

"Yep." I move over to the computer on my desk and boot it up.

"Good." Relief washes through his tone. "Did you check the security cameras to make sure the perimeter was safe?"

I click a couple of keys, and the cameras pop up on the screen. "Doing it now."

"Okay, let me know when you know everything's okay."

"Working on it," I mutter as I go through the cameras and

the security system, making sure everything looks good and is working correctly.

"So, this guy … this Creepy Charles guy, all he told you so far is that some organization sent him to check on Zhara and run some tests on her?"

"Yeah, but that's enough to be concerned."

"Oh, I know. I'm just wondering why they're checking on her and what organization sent him. Because I was under the impression he was a rogue."

"He is. We saw the mark. But apparently, he's joined another organization. That is if he's telling the truth. Rogues like to lie."

"True." I scroll through some footage that the system has flagged, not too worried yet. Sometimes animals outside can set them off. "What about the rogue we caught in your apartment the other day? Have we learned anything from him yet?"

"No. And I don't think we're going to." He gives a short pause. "The boss came and took him."

Now I'm the one to pause. "Why? That's not usual protocol."

"I have no idea," Benton mumbles with a drop of worry in his tone, which makes me worried.

"Jett said that, before we knocked the rogue out, he said something about HR Guardian Agency being corrupt."

"Yeah, but rogues are always talking about shit like that," he reminds me. "And honestly, I think they believe it."

"I think they do, too …" I trail off as the footage opens up.

"What the actual hell is this?" I replay what I just saw, thinking I saw it wrong the first time. But nope, I see the same thing again.

"What's wrong?" Benton asks.

"Hold on ... I'll call you back." I hang up, grab my phone, and leave the room. Then I barrel up the stairway and run down the hall, heading straight for the guest bathroom that I saw Wilder take Zhara to while I was reviewing the security footage.

When I get there, Wilder is sitting on the floor outside, reading something on his phone. He glances up at me as I slow to a stop in front of him. He takes one look at my expression and jumps to his feet.

"What happened?" he asks, stuffing his phone in his pocket.

I point at the shut bathroom door. "Is Zhara in there?" I ask, and he nods. "Are you sure?"

Wilder nods again then points at the door. "If you don't believe me, press your ear to the door and hear for yourself."

My brows dip as I walk up to the door and press my ear against it.

On the other side, I can hear Zhara singing. The sound makes me smile.

"She has a really good voice," I state as I turn to Wilder.

"Yeah, she does." He fidgets with a leather band on his wrist that he always wears to hide a scar. "Why did you just run up here like you just saw a ghost?"

I slump against the door and shake my head. "Because I might have just seen a ghost."

His forehead creases. "What the crap does that mean?"

I lift a shoulder then shake my head. "I'm not sure, because the footage got a little fuzzy, but I think one of the cameras caught Zhara's mom creeping around near the forest behind our house this morning."

Wilder glances at the door behind me then inches closer, lowering his voice. "But Zhara's mom is dead."

"Is she, though?" I question. "Because you know as well as I do that, if she was part of the agency, there's a small chance that something may have happened, and our bosses may have just had to make things appear that way."

"But we're not even sure if her parents were part of the agency. Or, well, we haven't found any official proof."

"That doesn't mean it doesn't exist." I swallow hard at the realization.

What if Zhara's mom is still alive and has let her believe all this time that she was dead?

"We can't let her find out until we know for sure," Wilder mutters. "This will hurt her so badly if it's true."

"I know," I agree, crossing my arms. "But why would she be sneaking around our place? Zhara wasn't even here at the time."

"I have no idea, but we need to find out because, if her mom was part of the organization, it also means she could be a rogue."

"Or worse, she could be working for the same organization as Creepy Charles, who apparently was sent to check on Zhara and do some tests on her."

Tests. I hate the word. It reminds me of the time when I was in the experimental facility. Not that I can actually remember being there. None of the test subjects that were rescued can. And while sometimes I wonder what I saw while I was there, what happened to me, sometimes I'm grateful that I can't.

"We need to look into this ASAP," Wilder states. "I'm

going to go check out the area and see if there are any clues that were left behind."

"I'll stay here and review the footage again and make sure it was her." I sink to the ground and open up the app that gives me access to my home security.

I'm not a fan of using my phone to review the footage, because it doesn't have as many features as my computer does. But I'm not about to leave Zhara alone when we don't know who that was creeping around in the forest.

No, I'm going to keep an eye on her until I know she's safe. And maybe even after that.

TEN

THE WOMAN ON THE SCREEN

TAKING A SHOWER FEELS GOOD, and not just because I'm covered in mud, but it's also relaxing. I didn't realize how much I needed to relax until I was standing under the stream of warm water that's currently pouring down from the showerhead in Jackson's massive bathroom. Seriously, his bathroom is the size of the entire upstairs of my house. Not that my house is small; Jackson's house is just that massive.

I stay in the shower for probably longer than I should, scrubbing down my skin and washing my hair with Jackson's body wash and shampoo. By the time I'm finished, I smell like him.

I breathe in the scent as I shut off the shower, open the door, and reach for a towel. Once I get all wrapped up, I pad over to the counter and pick up the clothes that Wilder gave me before I came in here.

When he handed me one of Jackson's shirts to wear, I didn't really think too much about it. My mind must have been too distracted by the wide hallways in the house, the glittering chandeliers, and the artwork hanging everywhere. But now that I'm alone without anything to distract me, the bigger picture is opening up. And by bigger picture, I mean I have to put on only a shirt and wear it in front of the guys.

I frown as I pick up the button-down shirt. "Why didn't I ask for a pair of pants? Then again, I doubt any of his pants would fit me. Still ..." My frown deepens as I take off the towel, slip my arms through the shirt, and button it up.

The hem reaches me mid-thigh, which is longer than most of the shorts I wear, so I'm not sure why I'm freaking out over this.

I suck in a huge breath as I stare at my reflection in the mirror. "Don't be a wimp, Zhara. You wanted to change who you are and that means trying things that might scare you."

I roll my eyes at myself.

Leave it to me to be afraid of wearing a shirt in front of a couple of guys. After everything that's happened, this should seem easy. I mean, I just learned I may have been adopted after spending my earlier life in a drug experimental facility. So this should be a piece of cake.

Sighing, I muster up every ounce of courage I have and walk out of the bathroom. And I'm instantly greeted by Jackson falling backward and landing on my feet. He must have been leaning against the door.

He greets me with a charming smile as he lies on the floor, staring up at me. He still has on his muddy clothes, making me wonder why he hasn't changed yet.

I tug at the hem of the shirt, feeling self-conscious. "What're you doing on the floor?"

"Waiting for you, silly." He sits up then pushes to his feet, turning to face me. His eyes scroll up and down my body.

"Not to sound totally cliché, but you look really good in my shirt."

I pull on the bottom of the shirt again. "Thanks. I'm not used to wearing so little, though."

He gives me a once-over again then grins. "Well, you definitely should." His grin widens as heat floods my cheeks. "Jesus, if I didn't know any better, I'd think you were secretly trying to kill me."

"Why?" I ask.

He just chuckles and shakes his head before draping his arm around my shoulders. "Come on; there's a couple of things I need to do before I can take a shower and change out of these muddy clothes."

"Okay." Confusion continues to swirl through me as he steers me down the hallway and toward the stairs. "What're we doing exactly?"

"Checking on the security cameras."

"Oh. Are you worried about something?"

He shakes his head as we reach the top of the stairway. "No. It's just protocol."

I nod like I understand, but I don't. I hate this—always feeling confused. It makes it feel like secrets are always hovering over me and at any moment one could drop right in front of my feet.

"Where's Wilder?" I ask as I peer around at the artwork hanging on the dark blue walls.

"He went to check on a couple of things," Jackson replies vaguely. "He'll be back soon, though."

"Is everything okay?"

"Yeah, we usually check around the house and yard after we've been gone for long periods of time, just to make sure everything is secure."

"That makes sense." At least, I guess it does.

He smiles like I'm completely amusing. I wish I knew why.

"It's the downfall of having such a large house." He gestures at the domed ceiling above us. "It draws attention, which is why I picked it out—because it was in the middle of nowhere. But there's still been a couple of times when we've had break-ins. And the security cameras have blind spots, so they don't always catch everything."

"You've had break-ins? In Honeyton?" As soon as I say the question aloud, I shake my head. "You know what? Forget I said that. After everything I've learned about this town over the last handful of days, I should know by now that it's not as safe as I thought."

"You're always safe with us," Jackson assures me, grazing the pad of his thumb along the bottom of my lip. "So stop frowning and relax."

"I'm trying." I sigh. "But it's hard when my mind is still stuck on that stuff I learned earlier today."

"I know," he says with understanding. "Don't worry, though. When we go shopping for your dress, you won't be able to think of anything else, because Wilder won't let you."

I angle my head to the side. "Why?"

"Oh, you'll see," Jackson assures with a devious grin.

Maybe I should be worried but, for some reason, I'm not. Well, not about the shopping part. Everything else, though, has me on edge.

"So, when we go to this masquerade, what exactly will we be doing?" I ask. "I mean, we'll be undercover, right? But it's a party, so ... what do we do while we're there?"

He smiles, his eyes crinkling around the corners. "Party, of course."

I frown at that. The last time I went to a party, I failed epically. What if I fail again tonight? What if I blow the guys' covers?

"Relax," Jackson stresses. "You need to stop overthinking things all the time."

Is it that obvious I do? Apparently.

"Sorry. It's just kind of my nature. To worry, I mean. I've been trying to stop, but ..." I shrug. "Apparently, it's been engrained pretty deep into me."

"Have you always been like that? Or, did you start to worry more after your parents passed away?"

"I've always been kind of a worrier," I admit, tucking a strand of damp hair behind my ear. "It got worse after my parents died."

"That's how it was for me, too. Right after my adoptive parents died, all I ever did was worry," he confides.

"You were a worrier?" I question with a trace of surprise.

"Remember how I was right after Axel injected you with devil's kiss?" When I nod, he adds, "Well, that was how the old Jackson used to be. I got wound up about everything all the time. I had anxiety so bad that I almost got kicked out of the program. Thankfully, after I got help, I learned how to control it better. But there are times, like when you got injected, when I lose control over it for a little bit and have to find my way out of the panic."

"I know how that feels," I admit quietly.

"Yeah?" he asks, and I nod. Then he sweeps some of my hair out of my eyes. "If you want, I can teach you some exercises to help you get through those times."

"What sort of exercises?"

"Breathing techniques. Visualization exercises. It's really about making yourself aware that you're panicking and reminding yourself that you'll make it through."

"You make it sound so easy."

"It's not," he answers truthfully, which I appreciate. If he had said it was easy, I don't think I would've believed him. "But it is manageable."

"Thanks. And not just for saying that, but for listening to me and offering help."

"Anytime." He hugs me closer to his side. "That's what friends are for."

Are they? Because, from my experience with Taylor, that's never been the case. She's always pressured me to do stuff that sets my anxiety off, and then, when I panic, she either gets annoyed or mocks me, which never helps.

Jackson being understanding is a whole new territory for me, and it makes me feel … well, calmer inside.

"Hold on," Jackson suddenly mutters as he digs out his phone. Then he sighs when he reads the screen. "Benton has been texting me relentlessly."

"About what? Creepy Charles?"

As soon as the words leave my lips, I mentally chew my own butt out.

"You know what? Forget I said that. It's not really any of my business."

"Don't stress about asking questions." He dismisses me with a wave of his hand. "You're pretty much part of the team now, so you can ask questions if you want."

I appreciate him saying that but wonder if he'd answer all my questions if I did ask them.

"And to answer your question, it's not about Creepy Charles." He pockets his phone. "Benton is trying to come up with a plan for what we're gonna do to keep Tank and Ralpho from talking to you. While none of us want you to have to do that, we need to be careful that we don't piss anyone off. Or, more specifically, piss Drake off. Jett has actually been working on trying to figure out if it's Drake specifically who's requesting the little meetup, or if it's just Tank and Ralpho being asshats and pretending they're the bosses, when they're not."

"Drake's the boss, right?" I check to make sure I'm keeping up with everything.

"Actually, he's not," he replies as we reach the bottom of the stairs. "We don't know who the boss is. It's part of our mission to find out."

"So, then, why is Drake so important?" I ask, scratching my wrist.

"That is the million-dollar question," Jackson mutters, dazing off for a moment. "The thing we can't figure out is why Drake seems to have a lot of power, yet it's been told to us many times that he's not the head boss. In fact, his sole purpose seems to be his name."

"What do you mean by that?"

He glances at me as we step into the foyer. "Whenever the name *Drake* is said, it seems to instill fear in everyone. And none of us have ever met him. Honestly, some of the guys have speculated whether he exists at all, or if he's like a bedtime story that gets told to scare everyone into behaving. If that's the case, then whoever started the legend of Drake is doing a damn good job, because the stories I've heard about him are ..." He wavers. "Let's just say Drake sounds like a very unpleasant person to be around."

Worry rushes through my veins. "But, if it is Drake who wants to talk to me, and he actually exists—"

He places a finger over my lips. "I'm going to stop you right there, because that's not going to happen. We already have a plan, a distraction that's gonna happen if it comes to that."

I gulp down an uneven breath. "But, if he exists, then why does he even want to talk to me?"

He lowers his finger from my lips, worry briefly flickering in his eyes. "It could just be because you've been spending time with us, and he wants to make sure you're not a spy or something."

My eyes widen. "But, aren't I, kind of?"

He dithers. "Not necessarily a spy."

"But kind of?"

"Maybe."

"You're being very vague."

He lets out a quiet sigh. "I know. And I apologize for that. But it's not really my place to tell you all of our group's secrets." He steers me into an office that's across from the foyer. "One day, we all need to sit down with you and give you the details. But it needs to be all of us."

I wonder why but don't ask as he removes his arm from my shoulders and heads over to a desk where probably the biggest computer screen I've ever seen is perched.

"Let me check on the cameras really quickly," he says as he rolls up his sleeves. "Once I know everything's good, I'll take you up to my room, and you can hang out there while I shower. Wilder will be back soon, so he can entertain you." He clicks a few keys on the keyboard then glances up at me. "Do you like music?"

I nod, confused once again at his sudden subject change. "Um ... Yeah."

He taps on a few more keys. "Then you should have Wilder show you his music and instrument collection. It's fucking killer."

I think about my old guitar propped against my bedroom wall. Playing has been such a stress reliever to me.

I wish I had it with me.

"Okay, everything looks good," Jackson mutters, clicking the mouse. "I think we can go upstairs ..." He abruptly lets out a sequence of curses, his body going rigid. When his gaze darts to me, worry floods his eyes. "Zhara, I need you to stay in this room for a bit." He strides across the room toward me. "Whatever you do, don't leave this room, okay?"

My heart thrashes in my chest. "Why? What's wrong?"

"There's someone on my property who doesn't have permission to be here and who might be dangerous."

My fear skyrockets. "Who?"

"It's just ..." He blows out an exhale. "Look, I don't want to scare you until I'm sure I know who it is." He looks me straight in the eye. "I need you to trust me on this."

There's that word again. *Trust.* And, while I want to trust him, another part of me wants to know the truth. But, can I do that? Be a demanding person?

I'm still unsure as I part my lips, but I never do get to find out as a series of alarms sound off, interrupting me.

"Shit." Jackson places a hand protectively on my arm as he sweeps his gaze around the room. "Stay here, okay?" He doesn't look at me as he swings by me and rushes out of the room.

I wrap my arms around myself, panic flaring through me as I glance at the door then the window. Should I try to lock them—

A metal wall suddenly slams down across the window, covering the glass. The door then slams shut and the deadbolt clicks.

Locked in.

I'm locked in.

I should be relieved, right?

But I'm not. In fact, I'm panicking even more.

Hugging my arms tighter around myself, I hurry over to the computer screen to see if it's still showing a view of the cameras. The screen is black. However, when I move the mouse around, it clicks on, showing me several different camera views from inside and outside the house.

I start to lean forward to get a better look, but guilt causes me to pause. Should I really be snooping through this? After all, Jackson said to trust him.

I'm about to move away without viewing the footage when something bizarre captures my attention on one of the cameras.

A woman dressed in a white dress, her long, brown hair flowing down her back. She has no shoes on and her back is to the camera, so I can't see her face.

Who is she? A maid perhaps? Jackson never mentioned having a maid, but we've only been here for about an hour. Still, the outfit she's wearing seems a bit weird for a maid. Even stranger, the camera starts to static as the woman steps forward. And not just once, but every time she takes a step.

I click the mouse, thinking maybe something is wrong with the computer.

"Why the heck aren't you working?"

As the words leave my lips, the woman on the screen pauses, her body stiffening. Then she slowly turns her head and looks straight at the camera.

I just start to worry that perhaps I pushed an intercom button or something when I get a good look at her face.

Then, nothing else matters.

Nothing makes sense.

I blink and blink again, thinking I'm seeing things. But, nope. Her face stays the same.

My stomach drops, nausea twisting in my gut.

"Mommy," I whisper.

NO, I must be seeing things. Hallucinating. Maybe that devil's kiss messed me up worse than the guys thought.

But, hallucination or not, somehow the woman on the screen can sense I'm watching her, her gaze never leaving the camera as she turns around and tilts her head. My already racing pulse accelerates even more as she looks me straight in the eye. In reality, there's no way she can see me. At least, that's how it seems like it should be. But, after everything that's happened, maybe she can.

I promptly shake my head at myself. *No, she can't, Zhara. Because your mom really isn't standing in one of Jackson's hallways.*

Regardless of the plausibility, my mom remains on the camera, staring at me with her familiar eyes. Yet, they seem darker and more haunted than I remember.

"Who are you?" I whisper as I watch her on the screen.

She angles her head even more, bending in a weird angle, like straight out of a horror movie.

I start to step back when she takes off down the hallway, flashes of light making her come in and out of view.

What on earth is going on? It's like she's made of light, and *she's* the one flashing on and off.

Is this what a ghost looks like? Do I even believe in ghosts?

When she flashes off completely, I dart my gaze across the screen, searching for her. I can't see her anywhere.

Someone knocks on the shut door that leads into the room that I'm standing in. Then the doorknob jiggles.

I hold my breath as I back up, telling myself that I'll be fine. That the door is locked—

The door flies open, and a blast of wind gusts through the room. No, not wind. Smoke.

I gasp, fluttering my eyelids against the metallic smelling smoke and bring my arms up protectively in front of my face.

"You don't belong here, sweetie," my mom's voice echoes throughout the room.

I must be going mad.

I have to be.

Before I can arrive at a conclusion, the air grows metallic, stinging my eyes and polluting my lungs.

Dizziness overcomes me. Then I'm greeted by darkness.

TWELVE
THE MYSTERIOUS NECKLACE

"ZHARA, OPEN YOUR EYES." I feel warm hands mold around my cheeks. "Come on, cute girl; stay with me, okay?"

I know that voice.

Jackson.

He sounds weird, though. Worried and in pain.

As he skims his thumb along my cheek, my eyelids flutter open. I blink a few times before my surroundings come into focus. I'm in the room with the computer, and Jackson is leaning over me with his hands on my cheeks.

"Hey." Relief washes over his features. "Tell me what happened? Are you hurt?"

I sit up and wince as my head throbs. "Ow, my head's pounding." I press the heel of my hand to my forehead.

"That's probably from whatever the hell kind of drug they put in the air." Wilder steps into my line of vision and crouches in front of me. He has a cut on his forehead, and worry reflects in his eyes. "Are you okay?"

I nod, reaching out and lightly brushing my finger across his forehead. "Are you?"

He nods, a pucker forming at his brow. "I'm fine. It's you I'm worried about."

"Why? What happened?" I rack my mind for an answer, hazy images surfacing. But I must be misremembering things because my mom is in the images.

"We're not sure." Jackson removes his hands from my face and frowns. "When we came in here, you were passed out on the floor, the door was open, and the air was a bit smoky. I tried to look at the security cameras to see what happened, but they started static'ing out the moment I left you in the room." He brushes hair out of my face. "Can you remember anything?"

I swallow shakily. "I have some memories of what I think happened, but I'm not sure if they're real."

Jackson's forehead creases. "What do you mean?"

I stare down at my hands. "I don't want to sound crazy."

Jackson hooks a finger underneath my chin and tilts my head up to meet his gaze. "No one's going to think you're crazy. Trust me; Wilder and I have seen a lot of shit that doesn't seem like it should be real."

I believe him—I do—but still ... What I saw ... It ...

"I thought I saw my mom," I whisper. "On the camera. And then the door opened up, and I thought I heard her voice. But then this metallic scent filled the room, and I passed out, and ..." I sigh heavily. "I'm not sure what really happened."

Jackson and Wilder remain quiet while trading an indecipherable look.

"What is it?" I ask, worried they do think I'm insane.

They stare at each other for a moment longer before Jackson looks at me. "Earlier, I thought I saw someone who looked like your mom on the security cameras—it's why I left this room," he explains cautiously. "But I couldn't find anyone when I went to look. I thought maybe I was seeing things, but I couldn't figure out why. The metallic scent you smelled might explain it."

I'm not sure if I feel better about what he said or worse.

"What was it? The metallic scent, I mean."

"I'm not positive," Jackson says. "But there are some drugs that have metallic scents to them, and most of them cause hallucinations."

So, I didn't really see my mom? Part of me wants to cry.

"We don't know much about these kinds of drugs," Wilder tells me while rubbing his jawline. "And it's weird that you and Jackson would have the same hallucination."

"Yeah, you're right," Jackson mutters with confusion, as if this just occurred to him. "And, who would sneak into my house and do this?"

"My bet is a rogue." Wilder lowers his hand from his jawline. "And, while I hate to say this, the rogues seem to be going after Zhara. I mean, first, that Creepy Charles guy, and then this ... It can't be a coincidence."

"I know," Jackson agrees with his gaze on me. "We need to figure out a way to make Creepy Charles crack so we can get to the bottom of what's going on and figure out why the hell they're going after her."

They exchange another silent look then Jackson rises to his feet. "I'm going to go have a video chat with Benton and see if we can find a way to speed up the process of getting Creepy Charles to break and then I'm going to double check all the security to make sure no one is inside the house anymore. I know the front door was open and everything, but I want to be absolutely certain whoever was here left. And that there's no one else here. You wanna take Zhara up to your room while her clothes finish drying?"

Wilder gives him a salute. "Absolutely."

"You might wanna clean up the cut on your head, too." Jackson gives a pressing look at Wilder's forehead.

Wilder lightly touches the cut. "Yeah, I'm not even sure how that happened. I think a tree branch smacked me in the forehead or something."

"Why were you in the trees?" I tug at the hem of my borrowed shirt to cover up more of my legs.

"I was checking out the yard to make sure no one was hiding out there," Wilder replies, pushing to his feet.

"Oh." I tuck my legs under me then start to stand up, but dizziness takes over and causes me to stumble.

Jackson envelopes his arm around me, keeping me from face-planting onto the floor.

"I want you to take it easy until we can figure out what sort of drug was released into the air," he tells me as he steadies me. "Go hang out with Wilder and try to relax. Once I get done talking to Benton, we can go shopping."

I nod, and he offers me a tight smile before transferring me into Wilder's arms.

"I think we should have Ridge come here and check her out," Wilder tells Jackson as he slips an arm around my back.

"I'm fine," I try to assure them. "I'm just a little bit dizzy."

"We're still going to have Ridge check on you," Jackson insists, grazing his finger along my cheek, something he seems to do a lot.

Benton does stuff like that, too, but that's because I'm pretending to be his fake girlfriend. I'm not sure why Jackson does it. Although, he is a flirty guy, so maybe that's just what he does with everyone.

"It's important after what happened to make sure you're okay," Wilder adds, drawing me closer to his side. "Especially when we don't know what kind of drug the rogue used on you."

While I hate getting check-ups, he has a point. Plus, Ridge isn't a real doctor, so it's not as bad.

"Okay," I agree.

They both relax at that, and then we all leave the room, Jackson heading to a room across the foyer while Wilder guides me toward the stairway. We both remain quiet. Wilder seems distracted. So am I, unable to stop thinking about how real it felt when I thought I saw and heard my mom. How could it be just a hallucination? But it had to be.

At least, I'm convinced of that until I spot something shiny on the floor. Wilder notices it, too, coming to a stop and removing his arm from around my waist so he can pick it up.

"Is this yours?" He holds his hand out, showing me what the object is.

A silver, heart-shaped locket with a purple stone in the center.

My chest suddenly feels tight as I veer toward having a panic attack.

"N-no ..." I answer shakily. "But I know whose it is." When my voice catches, worry floods his expression. I'm sure my expression mirrors his. "It's my mom's."

He glances from the locket to me, surprise flickering through his eyes. "Shit. That means the rogue probably stole it from your house."

I shake my head, blood roaring in my eardrums. "It wasn't at my house."

A crinkle forms at his brow. "Then, where was it?"

"My mom was wearing it the day she was buried," I whisper, struggling to breathe evenly.

Wilder pales. "What?"

I nod shakily. "Yeah. It was her favorite necklace, so ..." I reach out and brush my fingertips across it, feeling the strangest pull toward it.

I've always loved the necklace though. It was gorgeous and unique, and I'd always been drawn to it, even though she never let me wear it. In fact, she kept it locked up, told me it was extremely old and had a lot of value. After she died, I wanted to keep it. But in her will she insisted she be buried with it.

"Then, how did it get here?" He's not really asking me. He's just stating a question aloud.

I shrug, anyway, and he stares at me, confusion seeming to consume him.

The same confusion consumes me as a couple of answers come to my mind as to why the necklace is here. Either someone stole it from my mom's grave or ...

My mom was really here.

THIRTEEN

THE STRUM OF A GUITAR

WILDER DOESN'T SAY anything as we wander down a hallway toward what I'm assuming is his bedroom. My lips remain sealed, too.

The house is quiet, silence encasing us, but inside my head is a ton of noise. Questions are cramming my brain, so much that my headache is worsening.

Why was my mom's necklace laying on the floor around the same time I thought I saw her on the security camera? The guys thought we hallucinated seeing her, but the necklace Wilder is currently carrying is very real.

"I don't know what to say," Wilder finally says as we slow to a stop in front of one of many closed doors lining the hallway. He glances down at the necklace then back at me. "While I can usually find an explanation for strange stuff like this, this one ..." He shakes his head, puzzlement etching his face. "This one has me puzzled as hell."

"Me, too," I utter, my throat feeling dry, which shows through the hoarseness of my voice.

"Hey, don't get too worried yet." Wilder dips his head and catches my gaze. "I know this seems crazy, and we don't have a logical explanation yet, but we haven't even started looking into it. Or, I should probably say, Ridge hasn't looked into it yet. But I've already called him, and he's on his way over to look at the security footage. He might be able to clear up the static so we can analyze the footage better. He'll probably also run some tests on the drug that was just used on you and Jackson to see if we can find out what it was."

"Do you think he'll be able to figure out who did this?" What I really want to ask, but don't, is that if he thinks Ridge will figure out if my mom was really here. But I can't utter those words aloud. I'll sound crazy if I do.

Honestly, I'm wondering if maybe I am crazy. If all the drugs I've been around lately have done something to me. It makes me wonder about my mom. If she was doing devil's kiss, did it affect her mind? She never seemed crazy or anything like that. But now that I think about it, there were times when she would seem dazed and distant.

"If anyone can figure it out, it's Ridge," he assures me, wrapping his fingers around the doorknob. Then he starts to push the door open but pauses. "If it's okay with you, I'd like to hold on to this"—he holds up the locket—"and give it to Ridge when he gets here so he can analyze it. There might be some residue or fingerprints on it."

I nod. "Yeah, that's fine." Honestly, until I find out what's really going on, I'm kind of afraid to touch it.

"Thanks." He pushes the door open, enters the room, and then gently places the necklace on a desk that's beside the doorway.

I tentatively follow him inside, sweeping my gaze along the

unmade four-poster bed, the dressers, the instruments. But it's the walls, the ceiling, the doorframes that really snare my attention.

All of it has been painted black, but Wilder—at least, I'm assuming it was done by him—has painted a mural of a massive oak tree, the trunk sprouting from the baseboards and tracing up the walls, the leafless branches stretching across the ceiling. And in the center, right beside the light fixture, is a full moon surrounded by shadows that seem to reach for the lonely looking tree.

I shake my head in astonishment, no words coming to mind that can describe the amazingness that is this room.

"Did you paint all this?" I ask, tearing my eyes off the mural, only to find him watching me curiously.

He nods, flopping down on a chair in the corner of his room and picking up one of the many guitars. "I did."

I watch as he positions the guitar on his lap. "It's good."

"It is?" he questions as he strums the strings of the guitar. "Honestly, I was thinking about painting over it." He plucks a few chords then glances at the tree. "I was in a weird mood when I did it."

"A lonely one?" I ask.

He stops playing, glancing up at me with his brow arched. "Yeah, that's actually exactly how I was feeling. How did you know?"

I shrug, peering up at the tree branches and the moon. "I don't know ... The tree and the moon look lonely. Like they're together, but still so far away." I crinkle my nose at myself. What am I doing? I don't know anything about art. "I probably sound stupid, don't I?"

He shakes his head, observing me closely. "No, not at all."

He sucks on his lip ring. "You know, you're nothing like I thought you'd be."

"Is that a good or a bad thing?"

"It's a good thing," he assures then hesitates. "Can I be real with you right now?"

I nod, fiddling with a button on my borrowed shirt. "Yeah, of course."

"Before we officially met, I kind of thought you were uptight. And the fact that you hung out with Taylor ..." He wavers, pulling a face. "Well, I just thought you'd kind of be like her."

"Oh." I'm not sure what to say to that.

A lot of people seem to like Taylor, but the idea that he thought I was like her doesn't sit well with me.

"Or, well, a quieter version of her," he adds. "You were always so quiet in class and around school."

"I sometimes get anxiety when I'm around a lot of people," I admit. "I've always sort of been that way. That's why I'm surprised you think I'm like Taylor, because she's always been this social butterfly."

"I didn't say I think you're *like* Taylor. I said I *thought* you were," he stresses. "I in no way, shape, or form think you are now."

"Oh."

"And that's a good thing. I mean, I know Taylor is your friend, but"—he pulls another face—"I've never been a fan of hers."

"Yeah, a couple of the other guys said that to me, too. It's weird to me because, from what I've seen, guys are always drawn to Taylor."

"Shallow guys are." He plucks the guitar strings with his

long fingers. "Contrary to popular belief, guys can be just as shallow and ridiculous as girls." He flashes me an amused smirk. "Take Jackson, for instance."

"Jackson's not bad. He actually helped me out after I ..." I fiddle with the button on the shirt again. " ... after I found out about my past."

"I know he did. I was just teasing you." He strums a few chords, playing a flawless tune with a calculating expression on his face. "I don't see you like that anymore. I realized after spending about five minutes with you that you are nothing like Taylor. That you're kind, caring, amusing and, honestly, pretty fucking adorable. But don't tell Benton I said that."

I cock my head to the side. "Why not?"

He shakes his head, a semi-amused smile on his face. "It's just better if you don't."

Even though I wish he'd embellish, I nod. "Okay, I won't."

He smiles then goes back to playing his guitar. His head is tipped down, strands of blond hair hanging in his eyes. At first glance, he's the portrait of perfection, but I can't help thinking about the scars on his chest and how uneasy he got when I noticed them.

I wonder what happened to him. What sort of pain he went through. Is he past the pain now?

After playing about half of a song, he stops thrumming the strings and glances up at me. "Do you play anything?" he asks, sweeping his hair out of his face.

I contemplate shaking my head and lying. After all, no one but my mom knows I play the guitar, but I'm not much of a liar, either.

"I can kind of play the guitar," I admit with a shrug.

"*Really?*"

"Yeah, but I'm not very good. And I've never had any lessons. I just play by ear."

He taps his fingers against the side of the guitar, considering something before patting the chair beside his. "Pick a guitar then come sit down. Let's play something together."

Is he being serious? He sure looks like he is.

I quickly shake my head. "I don't think that's a good idea. You're way better than I am, and I'd just mess you up."

He grins cockily. "Princess, I promise you that, no matter what you do, you're not going to mess me up." He plays the intro to an extremely complicated song. "I'm an excellent guitar player." He pats the chair again. "So, come on; let's play. It'll take your mind off stuff."

He's probably right. Playing always takes me to a much calmer place, even if I'm not very good at it.

"We can play any song you want," he tries to entice me even more then pauses. "As long as it's not a pop song."

"I'm not really into pop music," I divulge as I nervously pad over to his guitar collection.

While I can play the guitar, I know nothing about guitars. The one I have, I purchased at a yard sale.

"What kind of music are you into?" he asks, setting his guitar down.

I raise a shoulder, shrugging. "I listen to a lot of stuff."

His eyes sparkle with humor. "Except for pop music."

"Yeah, except for pop music." I redirect my attention back to the guitar selection. "I've just never been able to connect with it."

"Yeah, me neither." He pauses then gets up and moves behind me. "Here, use this one." He reaches over my shoulder, his chest brushing against my back as he grabs a guitar. It's an acoustic; that much I can tell.

I take it from him, turning to face him, aware of how close he's standing to me. My heart is racing in my chest at his nearness. But it always does that whenever one of the guys gets close to me.

Smiling, he doesn't say anything as he traces a path down the side of my face. Then he returns to his seat, collecting his guitar and positioning it on his lap. Then he lines his fingers to the strings. "So, what're we gonna play?"

Holding the guitar, I sink down in the chair beside his while mentally sifting through the songs I can play.

Holy crap, am I really going to do this? Am I really going to play with Wilder? Am I really going to play in front of someone?

"Um ... How about 'Autumn's Monologue' by From Autumn to Ashes?" I suggest, tracing my fingers along the guitar strings.

He gapes at me but quickly recovers. "Okay, that so was not the song I thought you were gonna pick."

"What did you think I'd pick?" I ask, rotating my body to face him.

He nibbles on his lip ring. "I have no idea, but ..." He shakes his head, observing me intently. "You really do surprise me, princess. That much I do know."

For the millionth time since I was brought into the guys' world, I'm confused.

He doesn't comment further, simply tuning his guitar a bit then lining his fingers to the strings.

I do the same then wait for him to do ... something. Truthfully, I'm not sure what I'm supposed to be doing since I've never played with anyone before.

"You want me to count us off?" he asks, and I nod. "Okay ... One ... Two ... Three ..." He plucks the strings. So do I. And just like that, I'm playing the guitar with Wilder, one of the most beautiful and artistic guys I've ever met.

If only I weren't playing to distract myself from the fact that my entire life might be one big lie. But, like always, I do get a bit of peace from my worrying thoughts because, like every other time I play, the music carries me away from being Worrier Zhara, Anxious Zhara, Boring Zhara, and the million other labels I've been stuck with over the years. There are no labels when I play. I just become the music.

I become Just Zhara.

I get lost in the rhythm, the beat, the feel, the music, but then I'm yanked back to reality as Wilder starts singing.

Holy mother of all unicorns, Wilder can freakin' sing! I mean, I knew he could play. People talked about it at school all the time. But this ... His voice ... is beautiful. And that's putting it mildly.

He must notice my shocked face because he cracks a small smile, continuing to sing until there's a pause in the lyrics.

"You should sing with me," he says as we both continue to play our guitars.

I promptly shake my head. "No way."

"Oh, come on." He juts out his pierced lip. "It'll be fun."

I shake my head again, half my attention on keeping up with playing the song. "Easy for you to say. Your voice is like ..."

"Like what?" he presses. "Come on; tell me."

"Amazing." I give an awkward shrug as I continue to play.

"Honestly, you're better than amazing, but I can't think of a word to describe it."

He grins. "I'll take amazing." Another pluck of the strings. "I bet I'd sound even more amazing if you sang with me."

"How can you say that when you've never heard me sing? Maybe I'm tone deaf."

"Nah. No one can play by ear like that and be tone deaf."

"There's no way that statement can be true."

"Let's find out." He waggles his eyebrows at me. "Come on; sing with me. I feel like I'm showing off—singing all alone. Which I am. But, still ..." He smiles, and it's the most contagious thing that I actually almost smile myself. Even with my mom's necklace sitting on the dresser only feet away from me.

I want to latch on to this moment for a little longer. Not live in the present again just yet. So, taking a deep breath, I say, "Fine. But don't blame me when you go deaf."

"So damn amusing," he mutters under his breath with a soft chuckle.

I'm unsure why he thinks I'm amusing, since I was being completely serious.

"Ready?" he calls out as we play the final chord of the song then swing back around into the intro.

"I guess," I grumble.

Why did I agree to this?

What the heck is wrong with me?

I should just not do it.

But, as the intro ends and the first verse starts, I find myself singing along with Wilder. And, in that moment, I wonder who I even am anymore. This girl who's playing guitar and singing along with this guy, she isn't the girl who spent years consumed by the idea that she had to be perfect. She isn't the girl who was obsessed with getting good grades or the girl who thought she had direction. I'm not sure she ever really did.

I stop overanalyzing myself for a moment and focus on playing.

Wilder has a trace of a smile on his lips as I sing along with him, but I can't figure out why. Probably because of my tone-deaf voice.

I'm fine with that right now. I'm fine with everything as we play for a few more minutes until the song ends.

Then the quiet sets in.

Reality sets in.

"You're good," he states as he props his guitar against the wall.

I set my guitar down, too. "Not really. But I like playing."

"I wasn't just talking about your guitar playing." He twists to face me so his knees are pressed against mine. "You can sing really fucking well." He holds up a hand as I part my lips in protest. "No, let me take that back. You sing *fucking amazing*." He casts a glance at the doorway. "I think Jackson will agree with me, too. Well, if he's been standing there long enough to hear you."

My eyes widen as I snap my gaze toward the doorway.

Sure enough, Jackson is leaning against the doorframe, wearing a fresh pair of jeans, a button-down shirt, and a thick leather band over his wrist. He's also sporting what looks like a pair of brand new Converse, and his hair is damp from just getting out of the shower.

"You were listening?" I sputter.

I mean, yeah, Wilder heard me, but he was also playing and singing with me. Had I known Jackson was watching, I wouldn't have played.

"I'm sorry," he says as he pushes away from the doorway and walks into the room. "I just heard you guys playing, and I didn't want to interrupt." He stops just short of me with his arms crossed. "Wilder's right, though. Your voice is beautiful."

I've never done well with compliments, so my cheeks flood with heat as I shake my head and look away.

"You know what, Wilder?" Jackson muses. "I think my compliment might be embarrassing her."

"I think you might be right," Wilder agrees with amusement.

"No, it isn't," I try to lie. Then, taking a deep breath, I force myself to look at them. "I just ... I'm not ... I don't know ..." I grimace, frustrated with myself. "I'm just not used to this."

"Used to what?" Jackson and Wilder say simultaneously.

I pick at my fingernails. "All of this. Hanging out with people. Singing in front of people. People watching me. I've always sort of been invisible. Well, except for times when I decided to do something completely out of my character, like go to Benton's party. And now I feel like all this attention is centered on me, and it's just ... weird." I dare a glance up at them and find them trading an amused look.

Then Jackson looks at me with his hands stuffed in his back pockets. "I hate to break it to you, cute girl, but you've never been invisible."

"At all." Wilder stretches out his legs and arms. "People notice you all the time."

"Only because they think I'm this Goody Two-Shoes, know-it-all," I mutter then sigh. "I'm sorry. I probably sound like I'm having a pity party right now and over the most ridiculous thing, especially considering what just happened."

Wilder places a hand on my bare leg, reminding me that

I'm still only wearing Jackson's shirt. "Neither of us thinks you're having a pity party. And, even if you were, we wouldn't care."

"With all this shit going on, it's more than justifiable for you to have a pity party." Jackson sits down in a chair beside me and rotates his body toward me, resting his arm on the back of the chair that I'm sitting in. Then he glances at Wilder, giving a discreet nod before fixing his attention on me. "However, that being said, you're with two of the most charming, amusing, and sexy-as-hell guys, not just in the group but in the world. So, if anyone can cheer you up, it's going to be us."

"We're also the least humble," Wilder adds with an eye roll then smiles. "He's right, though; we can totally distract you from your funk."

My gaze dances between the two of them. "How?"

A smirk touches Jackson's lips. "Well, I have a ton of ideas, but if I said most of them aloud, Benton would probably kick my ass."

"You guys say that a lot," I point out.

"That's because Benton likes to kick our asses a lot." Wilder winks at me then trades a grin with Jackson.

What they're smiling about is beyond me, but I don't dare ask, fearing whatever it is will probably make me blush again.

"So, unfortunately, we're gonna have to settle for a Benton-approved way to cheer you up." Jackson's lips tug into a grin.

"Which means shopping time." Wilder rises to his feet. "But before that can happen, you're gonna have to get dressed." His gaze deliberately scrolls up and down my body. "Unfortunately."

Jackson combs his fingers through my hair and grins. "Definitely."

Again, I feel overwhelmed, like I did when I was in the car and wedged between the two of them. But, only moments ago, Wilder had made me so comfortable that I almost forgot where I was.

I wonder if it's part of their job to be able to go from serious to flirty in the snap of a finger.

It makes me wonder what parts of them are real.

And that leaves me wondering if anything they do is real, or if it's part of the job.

It makes me wonder if *I'm* just part of the job.

FOURTEEN

KISSES & LIES

A HANDFUL OF MINUTES LATER, I'm standing in front of a mirror in the bathroom that I took a shower in, dressed in the clothes I was wearing earlier. My hair is a tangled mess of waves but, since I don't even have a brush with me, I'll just have to let it be. And I've never been one for wearing much makeup, but I really wish I had some lip gloss, because my lips are extremely dry.

What I really need is some of my stuff. I haven't heard from Alexis yet about our plan of what we're going to tell Loki, so I decide to text her to check in and see if she's figured out when she'll be able to get home. I also send Loki a message, telling him I'm going to be spending the night at Taylor's.

He responds almost instantly.

Loki: That's fine. Are you going to be home tomorrow morning? Nik has a game really early.

Guilt squeezes my chest. I'm going to have to lie to him,

and I hate it. It makes me realize that, while I've questioned a lot of traits about my personality, this part of me is real. That I do feel guilty about lying. I just wonder how much of it was ingrained in me and how much of it is just me.

Me: I'm not sure. I'll let you know soon.

Loki: Oh, okay. I hope you can make it. I know Nik really wants you to go.

Tears burn my eyes as I become painfully aware that I probably won't be able to go, not just to Nik's game but to a lot of family things.

I want to tell Loki everything right then and there, confide in him then ask him what he knows about my past. But, if he doesn't know anything, it'll be dangerous to bring him into this world.

And if he does know about everything ...

Well, that might crush me. And I don't think I can handle that right now.

Me: Me, too.

It's probably the vaguest text I've ever sent, but I can't bring myself to lie anymore right now.

"I'll deal with that in a bit," I tell myself as I slide my phone into my back pocket.

I'll deal with everything in a bit.

After I comb my fingers through my hair a few times, I leave the bathroom and head downstairs to the foyer where Wilder and Jackson told me to meet them once I was dressed. When I get there, however, I can't find them.

Voices float from inside the office, the room where I passed out and where I ...

I swallow hard as the images of my mom on the surveillance camera flash through my mind. I can recall them so clearly, and it's terrifying. Not only because I thought I saw my mom, but because she also looked strange, like she wasn't herself, but possessed.

"Zhara."

I blink the images away as Ridge appears in the office doorway. It's been over a day since I saw him. He looks like he hasn't slept much since then. Dark circles reside under his eyes, and strands of his brown hair are sticking up all over the place. I think he might also be wearing the same T-shirt and jeans.

"Were you up all night?" I ask as I make my way over to him.

He pushes his square-framed glasses up the bridge of his nose. "Kind of. I was working on hacking into something, and it took way longer than I planned. And then Wilder and Jackson called me and told me what happened, so I rushed over here."

"Maybe you should've taken a nap before you came over."

He dismisses me with a shake of his head. "This is way too important."

"Yeah, but sleep deprivation can be bad for your health." Not that I'm one to talk about being healthy, considering all the weird health issues I have.

"I'll get some rest soon, but first, I want to check you and Jackson out and look at that locket." He turns toward the office then pauses, looking back at me. "As long as you're okay with all of that."

I give a nod, though I'm not certain I am. But I need to be cooperative, or I'll never get answers.

He noticeably unwinds like he was afraid I was going to say no.

"Come on." He nods his head, signaling for me to follow. "My stuff's in here."

"Yeah, Zhara, go on so Ridge can play doctor," Wilder's voice floats from the room and is followed by a couple of snickers.

Is someone else in there?

When I enter the office, I get my answer.

Not only is Wilder and Jackson lounging on a couple of leather sofas, but Jett is sitting in the computer chair behind the desk. He's sporting a plaid shirt and grey beanie, and his arms are tucked behind his head, looking as relaxed as he always does. I still haven't figured out yet if he's relaxed all the time because he's always stoned or if he's just that way.

"I'm not playing doctor," Ridge tells him as he crosses the room and picks up a bag from off the floor. "Playing doctor would imply I don't know what I'm doing, when you all know that I do."

"Do we?" Wilder cocks a brow as he sinks back in the chair and crosses his arms. "Or do you just tell us you do?"

Jett raises his hand. "Oh, I know the answer to that. Pick me."

Ridge rolls his eyes while Jackson snorts a laugh.

Wilder grins, his mouth opening, but Ridge talks over him. "Jacks, Zhara, come with me. I think it'll be better if I do your check-up without the joking commentary."

Wilder pulls a face while Jett looks utterly confused.

"What'd I say?" Jett asks.

Ridge merely sighs then strides out of the room, heading to a doorway across from the office.

"Well, gentlemen"—Jackson pushes to his feet then sets down the cup of water he was holding—"it's time for me to go get poked and prodded by know-it-all McGee in there."

"That's what she said," Jett says then laughs at himself.

Wilder laughs, and Jackson rolls his eyes but smiles. Me? I try not to blush but don't succeed.

Luckily, Jackson walks over to me, laces his fingers through mine, and pulls me out of the room before anyone can remark on my flushed cheeks.

Before I exit the room, I notice Wilder staring at mine and Jackson's interlocked fingers. His forehead creases, and he frowns. But then he plasters on a fake smile and winks at me when he notes I'm observing him.

So weird.

Why are guys so weird?

"I'll make sure this doesn't take too long," Jackson says as he pulls me out of the room. "Sometimes Ridge can get carried away with stuff."

"It's fine," I tell him. "I want to make sure we're both okay."

He gives my hand a squeeze. "We will. But when it comes to Ridge, sometimes you have to remind him that he doesn't need to check everything three to four times. He gets kind of obsessive with stuff. Not that that's always bad. But sometimes it's not necessary." He smiles at me before stepping into another room with me in tow.

This room is much more spacious and has a cozier feel than the office. The ceiling is higher, the pale blue walls make the area feel brighter, and the furniture looks way more comfortable. A fireplace is on the far back wall, and a doorway is to the right that leads to some sort of attached room where I'm assuming Ridge is. There's also what looks like a bar area, which is a little weird since none of the guys are twenty-one.

Unless they lied about their age.

That thought occurs to me out of nowhere and makes nervousness bubble inside me.

What do I know about these guys, other than they work undercover and are trying to bring down a bunch of drug lords? I mean, sure, I went to school with them for the last couple of years, but what if that was an act?

"You don't need to be nervous." Jackson grazes his finger along the inside of my wrist. "Like I said, we'll make this quick."

"I'm not nervous," I attempt to lie.

Either my expression gives me away or my sweaty palms, because Jackson raises his brow in accusation.

Why, oh why, am I not a better liar?

"Okay, maybe I am a little bit, but it's not because I'm worried this will take long."

"Then, what is it about?"

"I don't know ... I just saw that bar over there and was wondering if ... if you guys are really eighteen, or if that's just part of your cover and you're really twenty-one."

Jackson drags his free hand over his mouth, I think to conceal a smile. "Yeah, we're eighteen." He lowers his hand to his side. "It's not that crazy uncommon for eighteen-year-olds to be able to get ahold of alcohol."

He has a point.

"Right." I feel so naïve. "I don't know why I thought that was weird. I mean, I know people drink while they're underage. It was just kind of weird seeing a bar in your living room, and then I realized I don't really know much about you guys, so ..."

"You know more about me than most do," he confides as he steers me over to the sofa. He plops down, pulling me with him, then stretches an arm along the sofa behind me. "And while I know I said I can't tell you everything yet, I want you to feel like you can ask me questions, okay?" When I nod, he smiles. "So, what's filling up that pretty head of yours?"

Pretty?

Do not flush, Zhara. Don't you dare. It's just how he is. A flirt. It doesn't mean anything.

"Lots of things," I admit, staring down at my hands. "But they're things I know you don't have answers to."

"Like what?"

"Like what happened today. And why my mom's necklace was on the floor of your house."

"Yeah, I wish I could give you answers about that, but I can't. Not yet, anyway. Hopefully, Ridge can figure out the mystery."

"I'll do my best," Ridge says as he enters the room from the doorway with a small black case in his hand. "I'm hoping there will be fingerprints on that necklace, but it's probably very unlikely." Ridge takes a seat in the chair across from us, sets the case on the floor, and then leans over to open it up.

"I know. But I'm going to keep my fingers crossed." Jackson removes his arm from behind me and slants forward, resting his elbows on his knees. "So, what tools are you using, Doc? Hopefully, no probing devices."

Ridge rolls his eyes. "No, no probing devices. Nice try at a joke, though."

"And nice try at a witty comeback," Jackson quips with a smirk.

"That wasn't me trying," Ridge insists as he retrieves a strange-looking rectangular device from out of the case. If I had to guess, I'd say it was a thermometer, but it has a lot of buttons and is much bigger. "If I was trying, I'd have succeeded." He flicks a grin at Jackson.

"Whatever, man." Jackson starts bouncing his knee up and down, like he has a bunch of restless energy inside him. Well, either that or he's nervous.

I assess him, the way he keeps fidgeting and bouncing.

"You're nervous?" I don't mean to say the words aloud. They just sort of slip out.

I'm about to apologize when Jackson confesses, "I hate everything that has to do with doctors. When I was younger, after I was rescued from, well, you know"—he scratches his wrist—"I had to be sedated every time my parents took me to the doctor."

"My mom never really took me to the doctor. I never really got sick, though. Or hurt." My lips pull into a frown. "Thinking about it now, I'm not sure how I didn't know there was something different about me. I mean, who doesn't get sick or hurt? That's not normal." I'm not normal.

That revelation punches me hard in the gut.

"No one really is," Ridge states as he pushes a few buttons on the device.

"I'm definitely not." Jackson thrums his fingers against his legs as he works to put a smile on his anxious-ridden face. "So, I guess you and I can be abnormal together." He sticks his knuckles toward me. "Fist bump for being weirdoes."

I can't help giggling as I tap my knuckles against his.

He grins, pleased by something, and even relaxes a smidgeon. "She giggled," he informs Ridge.

"I know. I heard," Ridge replies with a small smile.

"Why's that weird?" I wonder confusedly.

"It's not. We just haven't really heard you giggle very much. It's cute. You should do it more often." He sweeps a strand of hair out of my face, smiling when my cheeks warm.

Why does he keep looking at me like that?

Whatever the reason, it's making me feel all fluttery inside.

"So, who wants to go first?" Ridge asks, causing the fluttery feelings to fizzle.

Jackson's smile fades, as well. "I will," he begrudgingly volunteers.

"I can do it if you want me to," I offer, slipping my hands under my legs to keep from fidgeting.

He dismisses me with a shake of his head as he shoves up the sleeves of his shirt. "Trust me; you don't want to go first. Ridge's machines always take a while to warm up, so the first person that gets checked usually has to get double-checked."

Nervousness stirs inside me.

Just what exactly is he about to do?

We all grow quiet as Ridge holds the device and traces the sensor along Jackson's arm, as if he's scanning his body. Once the device beeps, he checks the screen.

"My machine's actually working pretty okay today," he informs us then looks at me. "If it's okay with you, I'll just scan you now."

I give an anxious nod then stick out my arm. "What exactly are you doing?"

Like he did with Jackson, he moves the device along my

arm. "I'm taking readings from off your skin to see if there's any sort of foreign residues on you."

"Oh." I lower my arm as he finishes the scan. "That sounds like it's straight out of a sci-fi movie."

The corners of Ridge's lips quirk. "Yeah, it kind of does, doesn't it?"

I nod. "Between that and what happened earlier with the ... stuff I saw on the surveillance cameras, I feel like I'm living in a movie or something. Like a sci-fi horror movie."

Ridge lifts his attention from the screen, his brows furrowing as he glances from Jackson to me. "What do you mean by that?"

I shrug. "I just mean that everything I've seen today doesn't seem like it should be possible."

"You mean because you thought you saw your ... mom?" Ridge treads cautiously.

I force down the lump welling in my throat and nod. "I know you guys say I probably was hallucinating, but she looked so real. Or, well, real but strange. Like she was moving really weirdly, and her body couldn't bend right. And she kept flickering on and off, like she was made of light or something ..." I trail off as Ridge and Jackson jump to their feet.

"Are you thinking what I'm thinking?" Jackson asks Ridge as he tugs down the sleeve of his shirt.

Ridge nods as he sets down the device. "It's pretty damn plausible and is probably a better explanation than both you and Zhara hallucinating the same thing."

Jackson yanks his fingers through his blond hair. "It'd also explain why the surveillance cameras shorted out."

"Yeah, it would. You said you first saw her in the bottom hallway, right?" Ridge asks, and Jackson nods.

"I'm going to go check on it." Ridge hurries for the doorway, and Jackson follows, his sneakers scuffing against the hardwood floors.

Unsure what I'm supposed to do or what's even going on, I stand up to follow them when Jackson backtracks.

"Come on, cute girl." He laces his fingers through mine. "We may have an explanation for what happened earlier."

He doesn't wait for me to comment, towing me with him as he strides for the doorway.

"You think you figured out why I saw my mom?" I jog to keep up with him as he hurries toward the stairway then veers right, down a wide hallway.

"I think so." He quickens his pace until he reaches the middle of the hallway where Ridge is standing, staring at the wall with his arms crossed and his head slanted to the side.

Ridge taps his finger against his bottom lip as he crouches down and stares at the baseboard. He remains that way for a moment then reaches forward and pulls out a tiny object that's wedged under the baseboard.

It's small, about the size of a button, and has a black, metallic exterior.

"Would you look at that." Jackson lets out a frustrated laugh. "Those goddamn sneaky motherfuckers."

"What is it?" I ask, inching toward them.

Jackson pulls me closer to his side then slips his arm around me, his scent touching my nostrils. "That, cute girl, is how we saw your mom."

Right then, Ridge flicks the side of the object and light illuminates from it, casting shadows across the walls.

No, not shadows. What looks like a hologram of a figure of a woman with long, brown hair and wearing a white dress.

"My mom," I whisper. "It was just a hologram." Although, it's really startling how realistic it looks as the holographic figure moves and sways.

I didn't think stuff like this existed, but I also didn't think experimental drug facility existed, so yeah ...

Ridge shuts the device off as he pushes to his feet. "It's a high-tech one, too, which makes me wonder how the rogues got ahold of it."

"Unless it wasn't the rogues who did it," Jackson mutters with a frown.

"Who else would do it?" Ridge asks as he stares at the device.

Jackson taps the device with his finger. "I'm not sure, but I bet figuring out where this came from might get us some answers. Also, we might want to check out the forest out because I'm pretty sure there's probably another one out there."

Ridge pockets the device. "I'll do that before I leave. And then I'll do some research on it while I wait for you guys' scans to come back. Then, I want to do a few more tests on you guys, I'll talk to you in a bit." He walks off without saying anything else, looking extremely distracted.

The moment he leaves, Jackson turns toward me. "Are you okay?"

"Yeah." My voice cracks, and I hastily clear it. "I'm just glad we figured out what was going on."

"Zhara," he says with a soft sigh. "It's okay to not be okay. And after what happened ... after thinking that maybe your mom is alive ..." He brushes his fingers along my cheek.

I swallow thickly, fighting back the tears. "It's not that I'm upset she's not still alive. Honestly, I didn't really feel any better thinking she may have been, because that would've meant she's been alive this entire time and just let us believe she wasn't." I suck in a shaky breath as tears burn in my eyes. "But, I guess a tiny part of me kind of latched on to the possibility that maybe she was, and that part feels a bit crushed right now." A tear manages to escape my eye.

I reach to swipe it away, but he beats me to it, sweeping it away with the pad of his thumb. Then he leans forward and presses his lips to my cheek, giving me a soft kiss.

"Everything's going to be okay," he whispers. "We'll get you through this." He presses another gentle kiss against my face, this time on the corner of my lips.

My heart does that fluttery thing again, and I feel a bit dizzy.

I wonder if this is from the drugs still lingering in my system.

When he pulls back, he sketches a path down the side of my face. "We should go shopping. I know it sounds a bit ordinary right now, but I think that might be good for you."

I nod. "Okay."

Smiling softly, he takes my hand then leads me down the hallway toward the office.

Questions flood my thoughts, and one in particular plagues my mind more than the others.

"I still don't get how my mom's necklace ended up here," I finally say the question aloud. "I mean, that was real."

"It was probably put there by the same person who snuck in and put the holograms around my house."

I cringe, thinking about how the person got the necklace. The term *grave diggers* pop into my thoughts.

"And how they managed to do that without my security alarms going off is beyond me," Jackson adds with frustration. "But I double checked everything, and the house is completely clear."

"Maybe they've been in your house before and knew the layout," I suggest.

"Yeah, I've thought that, too, but hardly anyone is allowed in my house." His brows knit. "I also wonder how they knew we were going to be here, unless ..." His throat muscles work as he swallows hard.

"Unless what?" I urge him to finish.

He gulps audibly as his gaze fastens with mine. I can see the panic in his eyes, the worry, and I feel it radiating through me.

"Unless someone from the program is helping whoever did this." His fingers tighten around mine. "Well, either that or we've been bugged. Either way"—he shakes his head, his jaw ticking—"we need to find out what's going on. And quickly. Because, if we have been bugged ... then everything we do and have done ..." He trails off, not finishing.

But he doesn't have to.

I already get the gist of what he wants to say.

That everything we have done and are about to do could be overheard by the people who are currently trying to get ahold of me for whatever reason. Which means the guys' covers could be compromised if we're not careful.

"Let's go shopping, okay?" He gives me a pressing look, silently telling me to be careful about what I say.

Nodding, I walk with him down the hallway, pretending that everything is okay.

That I'm okay.

Pretending.

I'm starting to get good at it, but I'm still not sure if that's a good thing.

FIFTEEN

THE RARENESS OF ANSWERS

AFTER WE DISCOVER the hologram device, we head back to the office. As we arrive in the foyer, Ridge is hurrying out the front door.

"He didn't take the necklace with him," I inform Jackson, unsure if Ridge is supposed to or not, but it seems like something I should mention, just in case.

"Shit," Jackson curses then slips his fingers from mine. "I'll be right back." He jogs for the front door, pulls it open, and rushes outside, calling, "Ridge, hold on a damn second. You're getting so caught up in this that you're forgetting stuff."

"What's going on?" Wilder appears in the doorway of the office with his lean armed crossed over his chest.

I twist to face him. "Ridge forgot the necklace."

"Why's he even leaving?" Jett wonders, stepping up beside Wilder. "I thought he had a bunch of tests to run on you guys."

My lips part to tell him about the hologram, but then I close my mouth, wondering if I'm supposed to talk about this.

Wilder's brows dip. "What's that look for?" he asks me.

"Um ..." I struggle with what to tell him and end up just standing there, staring at him stupidly.

"I think she's broken," Jett jokes, resting his elbow on Wilder's shoulder. "Just kidding, Zhara. But for reals, why do you look so completely confused?"

"Because I'm not sure what I'm supposed to say," I mumble with a sigh. "Or what I'm allowed to say."

Jett straightens, lowering his elbow from Wilder's shoulder. The two of them frown at each other, having a silent conversation with their eyes.

"Understood," Jett says then faces me and grabs hold on my hand. "Come on; let's go out to the car." He doesn't wait for me to reply, pulling me with him as he bounds off down the hallway.

I cast a glance over my shoulder at Wilder and find that he's now following us.

"*I'll be there in a minute,*" he mouths with a reassuring smile.

Nodding, I twist back around and walk beside Jett, noting how much easier it is to keep up with him, his steps slower and less rushed than the other guys.

"Why are we going this way?" I ask as he guides me down a hallway and into a washroom. "Isn't the car parked out front?"

"We're not having Mable drive us to the store." Jett pulls open a door that's across from us. "We need to have some privacy, so we're going to drive ourselves." He walks through the doorway and into a garage.

The instant I step in ...

"Holy motherships," I whisper in awe as I peer around at

the ton of shiny, flashy cars filling up the enormous garage. "Who owns all these cars?"

"Well, technically, Jackson does." Jett flips on the light with his free hand, then pulls me with him as he walks farther into the garage and past the rows of cars. "But he lets us borrow them whenever we need them. Well, except for Lily. No one's allowed to borrow her."

"Lily?" Is this some sort of stoner talk happening right now?

"Yep," Jett replies.

When I continue to stare at him in perplexity, he grins then strolls by a line of cars, coming to a stop in front of a baby blue Chevelle. Jett lets go of my hand then and gives an exaggerated gesture at the car. "Zhara, I'd like you to meet Lily, the car none of us are ever allowed to touch."

"She's really pretty," I say. "But, why aren't you guys allowed to touch her?"

"Because it was Jackson's dad's car," Jett replies quietly, sounding more serious than I think I've ever heard him. "He doesn't even drive it himself."

That's so sad that I almost feel like crying.

"But anyway ..." Jett covers his mouth and clears his throat then turns back toward where the rest of the cars are parked in rows. "Go ahead and pick."

I gape at him. "You want me to pick which one we're going to drive?"

He lifts a shoulder, stuffing his hands into the back pockets of his jeans. "Yeah. Why not?"

Now I'm the one to shrug. "I don't know ... Because I know nothing about cars."

He rubs his scruffy jawline. "Okay, well, what's your favorite color. And please don't say pink or this won't work."

"It's not pink," I promise. "Honestly, I don't really have a favorite color."

"Seriously?" he asks, and I nod. "Dude, we so need to fix that. Everyone has to have a favorite color." He pauses, contemplating, then his eyes light up. "Okay, imagine you're driving around in your favorite car. What color would it be?"

I'm still uncertain but do my best to visualize it. "Maybe dark blue."

"What an excellent choice." He winds around cars and comes to a stop in front of a dark blue one. "Zhara, I'd like you to meet Larry."

"This car's name's Larry?" Is naming cars a thing?

"Well, it doesn't really have a name, but I think Larry's really fitting."

I eyeball the car and figure out that it's a Dodge Challenger.

"You think the name's bad?" he questions.

I shake my head. "No, Larry's a good name."

"Is it?"

"Um ... sure ..."

He assesses me with a curious sparkle in his eyes. "Well, if you could name it, what would you name it?"

"I don't know."

"Try to think of one. Come on; it'll be fun."

"Um ... okay." I glance at the car again. "How about Stella?"

"That's a girl name," he states the obvious.

"It kind of looks like a girl," I say with a shrug.

His gaze skates to the car. "You know what? It kind of

does." He smiles at me. "Stella, it is." Then he swings around to the passenger side, opens the door, and gestures for me to get in.

I shuffle over to him and slide into the back seat, the leather cool against the backs of my legs. He climbs in with me, shuts the door, and then gets situated in the seat.

Quiet settles between us, and he seems content with that.

Well, I assume he does until he says, "You know, you're handling all of this pretty dam awesomely." He glances at me, and the almost constant, playful sparkle in his eyes is no longer there.

"I'm trying my best." I recline back in the seat. "It's a lot to take in."

"I think that might be the understatement of the year." He rotates toward me, bringing his leg up onto the seat between us. "It has to be hard. I mean, only a couple of days ago I was trying to teach you some bad girl skills so you could play the role of Benton's girlfriend. And now you're ..." He trails off, wavering.

"I'm what?" I wonder. "Because with everything that's happened, I'm really starting to get confused what role I'm supposed to play."

He offers me an adorable lopsided smile. "You'll still play the role of Benton's girlfriend, as long as you're cool with it. But I'm not sure what we're going to do about this meeting that's supposed to be happening with Tank and Ralpho tonight. I mean, we were already working on a plan to get you out of this. But with this thing that happened just barely, it's pretty clear someone is after you. And until we know who it is, I'm not sure if it's the best idea to just turn you loose at Drake's masquerade ball. But if we don't, I'm not sure what Drake will do." He frowns. "Honestly, what we fucking need is some answers."

I nod in agreement. "Answers would be really nice."

The passenger door is opened then, and Wilder starts to climb in.

"For sure," Jett coincides. "The problem is answers are usually rare. Questions, on the other hand, are everywhere."

"Dude, Jett; enough with the stoner talk," Wilder says as he shuts the door. Then he rotates around in the seat, looking at Jett. "While sometimes you can be insightful, you can also talk a lot of nonsense."

Jett gives a half-shrug, pulling his beanie off his head, strands of his brown hair sticking up everywhere. "Yeah? So? Nonsense can be insightful, too."

Wilder rolls his eyes, but smiles. "I sometimes feel like I'm in Wonderland when you're talkin'."

I giggle, causing both of them to smile.

"I love it when she giggles," Wilder states, pulling something out of his pocket.

"For sure." Jett sneaks me a teasing smile. "I don't think bad girls are supposed to giggle, though."

"Really?" I question, watching as Wilder takes his phone, taps the screen, and holds it out in front of him. Whatever app he has open beeps a few times then the screen flashes green.

"Nah, you can giggle all you want," Jett tells me, draping an arm along the back of the seat. Then he looks at Wilder. "I take it we're good."

Wilder sets the phone down on the console "Yep At least we are in this car. Not sure about our house anymore. Or any of our other places."

I'm assuming this means that Jackson informed him the

place may be bugged. And apparently, Jett was brought into the loop, as well. I'm not sure how, other than maybe they were texting each other.

"I still can't believe our places could be bugged," Jett murmurs. "I mean, how did anyone get passed Ridge's security? Not just the one he installed in here, but at our hideout too. Because according to Ridge, those cameras didn't pick up anything either."

"I have no fucking clue," Wilder mumbles. "Maybe if we knew the whole story. Because, so far, Jackson has been really vague in his texts. Probably for a good reason." He turns in the seat to look at me. "Princess, you mind filling us in? I mean, why did Ridge run out of the house like it was on fire? And what did you guys find out that lead Jackson to believe we've been bugged?"

I hesitate because, for one, it's weird that he's looking to me for answers, and two ... "Is it okay to talk about this? Because Jackson acted like I needed to not talk about it."

"You're good in here," Wilder assures me. "That thing I just did on my phone checked for bugs. There's none on us or in the car."

"Oh, okay." I start filling them in on what happened with the hologram.

By the time I'm finished telling them, Jackson is climbing into the car.

"You filled them in?" he asks, glancing at me.

I nod. "Is that okay?"

"It's perfectly okay," Jackson says as he turns the key and revs the engine. "In fact, I'm glad you did." He winks at me from the rearview mirror. "It saves me some time having to do it myself." His blue eyes bounce from Wilder to Jett. "I have

Benton looking into the bug situation. He's supposed to get back to us soon. We're probably going to have to check all our houses, hideouts, and places we hang out. And we need to find out who did it and for how long, because there's a risk that our cover could be compromised."

"So, what do we do until then?" Jett asks, retrieving a lighter from his pocket and flicking it on and off, seeming fidgety. "If we're at risk for our cover being blown, then there's no way we can go to the party tonight."

"Until we know for sure what's going on, we're just going to keep moving forward. Benton will give us some answers before then, and then we'll go from there. For all we know, mine and Wilder's house is the only place bugged, and we rarely have business talk in there. And we already have Creepy Charles being interrogated. He could be one of a two-person party in this."

"Or he could be one of a ten-person party," Wilder states as he cranks off the air conditioning. "That's a really risky game to play, Jacks."

"I know, but ..." Jackson blows out a sigh. "I just really don't want to be pulled off this assignment. We've all put so much work and time into it, which is why Benton thinks we should keep this on the lowdown until we have more details. He doesn't even want the boss knowing."

"I agree with that." Wilder folds his arms across his chest, staring out the window. "If he ever finds out that we left him out of the loop, though, he'll be pissed."

"It's better than telling him there's a possibility we might've been bugged and he immediately kicking us off the job," Jett tells him. " 'Cause, you know he will."

They sink into silence for a moment.

I feel awful, knowing the only reason they're in this position is because of me.

"I'm sorry," I say quietly, eliciting puzzled looks from all three of them.

"For what?" Wilder asks, twisting in the seat.

"For causing problems for you guys," I say, growing fidgety the longer all three of their gazes remain on me. "If it weren't for me, your covers wouldn't be at risk right now."

Frowning, Wilder looks from Jett to Jackson, who shakes his head then turns in the seat to face me.

"First of all," Jackson says, "you're only here because we brought you into our world. And second, the whole point of our jobs is to bring down the bad guys and protect the innocent, and you're innocent in all this, cute girl. That much we do know."

"You're like one of the most innocent people I've ever met," Wilder stresses.

I frown at little at that. Getting called innocent is basically as bad as being called cute. Not that it matters right now.

"Aw ... don't pout." Jett reaches over and pushes my jutted out lip back into place. "It's kind of cute that you're so innocent."

Jackson lets out a low laugh. "Yeah, she doesn't like being called cute."

"Then why the hell do you call her cute girl?" Jett asks, gaping at him.

Jackson shrugs, amusement glittering in his eyes as his gaze flits to me. "Because she is." He grins at me when I glare at him then turns back around in his seat, pushing the button of the garage door opener, and one of the three doors starts to raise up. "And it could be worse. I could be calling her pink cheeks." He throws a smirk at Wilder.

"Whatever. It wasn't that bad of a name," Wilder protests. "Besides, I gave her a new one, anyway."

"Hmm ... Why haven't I given her one?" Jett asks with a musing look on his face.

"I don't know, bro." Jackson shakes his head then sneaks a glance at Wilder, putting his fingers to his lips and mimicking taking a drag off either a cigarette or joint.

Wilder nods then rolls down the window. "You sit on that, Jett, and let us know what you come up with."

"Okay, on it." Jett nods then turns and assesses me.

Great. Is he going to do that the entire drive?

"So, Ridge is looking into the hologram thing?" Wilder asks Jackson, changing the subject.

Jackson nods, craning the wheel so he can steer around the other vehicles and out of the garage. "Yeah. He took off so damn fast, though, that he almost forgot the necklace. I love Ridge to death and everything, but sometimes he gets so caught up in the job that he forgets other stuff."

"Like eating and showering," Wilder remarks as he fastens his seatbelt.

"I'm gonna figure out a good nickname for you," Jett whispers. "But it'll take some time."

He tears his attention off me and slides forward, resting his arms on the back of the seat and joining in on Wilder and Jackson's conversation. "Remember that one time he didn't shower for like a week 'cause he was trying to hack into some files? He started smelling so gross that Benton had to talk about it with him."

Wilder's face twists in disgust. "Yeah, that smell still haunts my nightmares."

"We need to keep an eye on him," Jackson states as he drives out of the garage and onto the paved driveway that leads to an iron-gated entrance. Beside the entrance is a screen mounted into a brick wall. "I can tell he's heading to that place already."

"I think it'd help if Xavier and Benton can get some info from Creepy Charles." Wilder flips down his visor. "If they can get him to confess that it's the rogues going after Zhara, it'll eliminate the need to look into it more."

"Although, it'll put an entirely different problem on our hands," Jett points out. "If the rogues are after her, they'll probably keep coming after her until we can get to the bottom of why and deal with the problem." He taps his fingers against his knee. "You know, I know her sister Alexis has another group after her besides the rogues; do you think maybe the same group could be after Zhara?"

"That wouldn't explain why Creepy Charles was after her." Jackson pulls the car up to the closed gate. "Because he's definitely a rogue. And then you have the rogue that broke into the apartment, although I'm not sure if he was there for Zhara or not. Honestly, my bet is Ridge is going to call and inform us that the hologram was created by rogues." He rolls down the window, pushes a button on the screen, and the gates swing open. Then he returns his hand to the steering wheel and drives out onto the road.

Clouds are still lingering in the sky, but sunlight is trickling through the cracks and trying to dry up the puddles covering the land. I used to love splashing in puddles after it rained, but that was back when I was younger, back when life consisted of rainbows and sunshine and everything light. Now, everything feels as shadowy as the clouds above.

"I hate to say this," Jackson says as he speeds up the car. "The rogues ... They could be after her because of her past. You know, some of them believe that the people rescued from the experimental drug facilities are ... bad." He gives me an apologetic look from the rearview mirror. "Not to frighten you or anything, cute girl. And we all know you're not bad. Unfortunately, not everyone has that same viewpoint."

"But the rogue's not coming after you," I point out. "And we kind of have the same past."

"I know." Jackson wets his lips with his tongue. "But the program has also worked really hard to cover up my past."

I struggle not to frown. "Oh."

"We should do that for her," Wilder suggests. "I mean, after we figure out why this particular group of rogues is coming after her and get the problem taken care of, we should put in a request to have her past cleaned up."

"I like that idea." Jackson flips on the blinker and makes a turn onto the highway, taking us away from the hills and toward town. "Just as long as Zhara is cool with it?"

All three of them look at me, and I have no clue what to say

"What does *cleaned up* mean exactly?" I ask, hoping I don't sound stupid.

"It means that files of your past, particularly from the time you spent in a drug facility, will be erased." Jackson slips on a pair of sunglasses. "That way, no one else can find out you were ever there."

"That doesn't sound too bad." Could it be that easy? Just wipe away the bad parts of my past and start over?

But, would that also mean I wouldn't be able to learn more about my past? Why my parents adopted me? Who I really am? Mia M.? Where I come from? Why I was ever in an experimental drug facility to begin with?

Do I want to learn the answers?

Do I want to know the truth?

If only I knew the answer. But, like Jett said, answers are rare.

SIXTEEN

SWEET PROMISES

ABOUT TEN MINUTES into the drive, Jackson receives a call.

"Hey," he answers, then gives a short pause. "Can I put you on speakerphone? We're in the car heading to the store right now." Another pause. "Okay, cool." He places the phone on the console then taps the speaker button. "All right, everyone can hear you," Jackson says, returning his hand to the steering wheel.

"Hey." Benton's voice flows through the speaker. "So, I have some good news and some bad news."

"How very cliché of you," Jett remarks with a clever grin.

Benton lets out an exhausted sigh. "Jett, I'm cool with you smoking sometimes, but you gotta let up on it."

They've all mention Jett's smoking a lot of times, making me wonder how often he does it and if maybe he has a problem. Loki used to smoke a lot in high school and in college, and I once heard my dad tell him he was fine with Loki getting high on occasion, just as long as he did it responsibly and didn't overdo it. I wasn't sure what he meant by that at the time, but now I'm wondering if maybe Loki was getting high too much.

Now that I think about it, he did seem stoned all the time whenever he'd come home on weekends to do his laundry. Not that he does that now. No, Loki is Mr. Responsible now.

"I'm fine," Jett says with a roll of his eyes.

"Okay." Skepticism is evident in Benton's tone, but either Jett doesn't hear it or ignores it. "Anyway, back to why I called. Do you guys want to hear the good news or the bad news first?"

"Good," Wilder and Jackson say simultaneously.

I'm not surprised. They both seem like good news sort of guys; usually upbeat and positive.

"Okay," Benton starts. "Well, we had all of our homes and hideouts scanned for bugs and the only place the scanner could find any is you guys' place."

It's still so weird hearing them talk like this, even after everything that's happened. Bugs? Scanners? I have to wonder what other kind of high-tech spy devices exists.

"That's good," Jackson says, turning off the air conditioning.

"Ridge also got back the tests he ran on you and Zhara," Benton continues. "And the drug he found on both of you was just a mild sedative that has no long-lasting side effects. It's also a drug commonly used by rogues in those stupid smoke bombs they use."

"So, does that mean the rogues were behind what happened at my house?" Jacksons asks, resting his arm on the windowsill.

"We think so. Although, we could be certain if we could

get Charles to talk. But, so far, the guy refuses to cooperate," Benton says. "The guy is one of the most annoying rogues I've ever met. Some of the shit he's saying is so damn foul that I can't ..." He trails off.

"What's he saying?" Wilder presses.

"I'd rather not talk about it while I'm on speakerphone," Benton replies. "Honestly, I don't want to repeat it at all."

A beat of silence ticks by, and I catch Jett and Wilder's gazes traveling in my direction.

Wait? Does Benton not want to talk about it because I'm in here?

"So, that's the good news," Benton says. "Now for the bad news, which is actually about that hologram and necklace you guys found. Ridge says the hologram's ID number is untraceable, so he can't use that to figure out who it belongs to. And as for the necklace, he dusted it for fingerprints and the only two he could find on it were Wilder's and Zhara's, probably because you guys are the ones who found it, so that's not going to help us at all either."

"So, we still have no fucking clue who's going after Zhara," Jackson states with a grimace, "which means we don't know the reason behind what they did today."

"No, but personally, I think it's rogues," Benton informs us. "It'd make sense, considering Charles was tailing her and he's a rogue. I just don't know the why. Or who they're working for."

"Wait ..." I say, surprising myself and them—I'd been so quiet up until that point. "I thought rogues worked for themselves? That they were people who left or got kicked out of the program."

"They are," Benton tells me. "But, while some are simply a

part of a group that wants to get back at the program, there are some who have gone a bit darker and started working for … well, I guess the best way to say it is they work for the bad guys."

"And since there's a lot of different bad guys in this world," Jackson adds, "even if we find out rogues are the ones going after you, we still need to find out which bad guys they're working for to get to the bottom of what they're trying to do to you."

"My bet is it has to do with her past," Benton mutters. "I just don't know why."

Anxiety takes a hold of me. So, a group of people that potentially work for a group of bad guys is tailing me and doing things to make me believe my mom is still alive. Why? What's the point?

"Hey, we'll figure it out," Jett says, reaching over and patting my leg. "We may not know a lot now, and I know I said answers are rare, but if anyone can get answers, it's us." He offers me a small smile.

I force my lips to turn upward, but it's difficult.

"He's right," Benton says. "We'll figure this out. Ridge is still working on some stuff, and Xavier and I are working on getting info from Charles. Until we figure out more, though, I want you guys to be careful."

"We always are," Jackson tells him, reaching for his phone. "Keep us updated, man."

"Wait. Can I talk to Zhara for a moment before you hang up?" Benton quickly says before Jackson can hang up. "And not on speakerphone."

"Um … sure." Puzzlement creases Jackson's features as he picks up the phone and hands it to me.

Wilder and Jett look just as confused. I feel that confusion, too.

Why does he want to talk to me privately? Did I do something wrong?

I take the phone from Jackson and put it up to my ear. "Hello?" I say, chewing on my thumbnail.

"Hey." Benton doesn't sound upset or anything, which makes me relax a little bit. "I just wanted to make sure you're okay. I barely got to talk to you before you headed off with Wilder and Jacks. And then the thing at the house happened, and I ..." He exhales loudly. "I'm so sorry that happened, sweetheart. I can't even imagine how awful that was—thinking you saw your mom."

"It's fine," I say automatically, an annoying trait I'm starting to realize might be branded into me.

"You can be real with me, okay?" Benton promises me. "I know there's no way you can be fine. It's okay, though, if you don't want to talk about it. It's also okay if you do. Just know that I'm here for you either way."

I find the moment so strange. Only a few weeks ago, I thought Benton was a rough, intense, bad boy. And maybe he is all those things. But he can also be really sweet, caring, and sympathetic.

"I think I'm okay with not talking about it right now," I tell him. "But thanks for the offer."

"Anytime." He pauses. "Are the guys being nice to you?"

I glance at Jackson, Wilder, and Jett. None of them are looking at me, but I have a feeling they're trying to listen. "Yeah, they've been really nice."

"Good."

Another pause, and I get the impression he wants to say something but is hesitating.

"Is everything okay?" I wonder, lowering my feet to the floor.

"Yeah, everything's fine." He briefly hesitates as voices rise in the background. "Shit, I have to go. Call me if you need anything at all, okay?"

"Okay."

We hang up after that, and I return Jackson's phone to him.

"Is everything okay?" Wilder asks, surveying me closely.

I nod. "I think so. He just wanted to know if I was okay."

"Hmm ... Did he now?" Wilder glances at Jackson, who elevates his brow.

Jett glances up at them, his brows puckering. "Why're you two looking at each other like that?"

Well, at least I'm not the only one confused.

"Because we love to stare longingly into each other's eyes," Jackson jokes, stuffing his phone into his pocket.

"You should try it." Wilder joins in on the joke then raises his voice to an exaggerated high falsetto. "Jacks has like the prettiest eyes ever."

I snort a laugh, and Wilder smirks at me.

"So, was that laugh because you thought I was funny?" Wilder asks me. "Or because you think the idea that Jackson has the prettiest eyes is funny?"

"Um ..." My gaze glides across the three of them, who are all looking at me. I try not to squirm. "It's because you're funny."

"Aw ..." Wilder presses his hand to his heart and looks at

Jackson. "Did you hear that, Jacks? Zhara thinks you have pretty eyes."

A flush spreads to my cheeks. "I didn't mean it like that."

Wilder cocks a brow at me. "So, you don't think his eyes are pretty?"

"No ... I just ... What I meant was ..." I grow flustered and can barely get any words to come out of my mouth.

"Come on, guys; leave her alone," Jett chimes in. I'm about to offer him a thankful smile when a sly grin creeps across his face. "We all know she thinks *I* have the prettiest eyes."

The three of them start to laugh but then grow quiet as all their phones start beeping.

They dig them out and frowns touch their lips as they glance at the screen.

"Shit, the boss is paying us a visit," Wilder mutters underneath his breath.

Silences wraps around us again. And it's an unsettling kind of silence.

I'm left wondering why.

Who is their boss and why does him paying them a visit make them all seem so uneasy?

SEVENTEEN

SYRUP AND WAFFLES

I REMAIN FAIRLY quiet for most of the drive, stuck in my own head, thinking about everything that's happened. The guys keep pretty quiet, too; Wilder texting on his phone, Jackson focusing on driving, and Jett staring out the window. I'm not sure if they're all worried about rogues, the job, or their boss visiting. Maybe a little bit of both.

When we reach the middle of town, Jackson pulls into a small shopping complex that has a couple clothing stores, coffeeshops, and restaurants.

"You had this place checked out, right?" Jackson asks Wilder as he parks the car in front of a clothing store, the display window decorated with mannequins wearing lavish dresses and fancy clothes that I could never envision myself wearing. Although, I'm unsure if that lack of vision stems from the old Zhara's mentality.

Wilder nods, unfastening his seatbelt. "I checked it out, and it's all clear. At least of bugs."

"Good." Wariness creeps into Jackson's expression as he

turns off the engine and eyes the store. "Is it even open? Because it doesn't look like it is."

"It is. Or, well, I called Jewels, and she's opening up just for us." Wilder tosses Jackson a smirk. "Yeah, I know. I've got some badass connections."

"Leave it to Wilder to have connections with a clothing store owner," Jett jokes as he tugs his beanie back on.

"Hey, personally, I like that connection. You just don't like it because you hate clothes." Grinning, Jackson throws a look at Jett's plaid shirt and jeans. "Obviously."

Wilder grins, too, pushing open the door and climbing out. "Sorry, Jett, but you're probably outnumbered on this one. At least with the crowd you're with."

Jett muses over something as he pushes the seat forward. "Hey, maybe Zhara is with me on this one." He elevates a brow at me. "What do you say, Zhara? Are you a girl that's into clothes or not?"

"Um ..." I glance at Jackson, who's watching me amusedly, and then back at Wilder, whose expression is begging me to agree with him. But the problem is, I don't know the answer. I mean, normally, I'd say no, but that's an instinctive response. "I don't know."

Wilder lowers his head, wisps of his hair hanging in his eyes as he looks at me, a smile playing at the edges of his lips. "You may not know now, princess, but trust me; after this ever-so-awesome shopping trip that you're about to embark on, you're gonna want to go shopping all the time."

I just smile because, truthfully, I don't ever see that happening, no matter what Zhara I am.

Jett laughs as he ducks his head to get out of the car. "I think she might disagree with you, man."

I slide across the seat to get out while Jackson grabs the keys and hops out, too.

"Maybe she does now but, trust me; I'll change her mind." Wilder offers me his hand.

I take it, and he helps me out. Then, without letting go of my hand, he bumps the door shut and starts toward the entrance to the store.

Jett seems oblivious to Wilder holding my hand, but Jackson's gaze briefly strays to our interlocked fingers, and a pucker forms between his brows. He hastily erases the look with a shake of his head then pulls open the entrance door, holding it open for us.

Jett enters first, then Wilder follows, towing me with him, while Jackson moves up beside me, walking close enough to me that his shoulder keeps brushing against mine.

The store is small but fancy, with mirrors lining the back wall near a seating area, a small table, and changing room. Glittering chandeliers decorate the ceiling and racks and racks of clothes cover everywhere else. Not a single person appears to be in here, including the storeowner

"It smells like waffles in here," Jackson remarks as he takes a deep inhale.

I sniff the air, too. "You're right; it does." My stomach must love that because it lets out the loudest grumble.

Jackson presses back a laugh, but Wilder and Jett chuckle.

"You hungry?" Wilder teases, tugging me toward him. "Or did you just eat a baby gremlin?"

"Sorry," I apologize. "I just haven't really eaten anything since earlier."

"I know that, which is why I had Jewels bring breakfast." Wilder stops near the sofas and gestures at a table covered with stacks of waffles, plates, syrup, and wineglasses filled with orange juice. "There's a catch, though."

My mouth practically salivates at the sight. "What's that?"

"No syrup near my dresses." A slender woman, probably in her mid-thirties, with long, brown hair, emerges from the back doorway. She's wearing a black, lace-tipped silk top, jeans, lace-up boots, and a sparkling necklace.

Wilder smiles at the sight of her then releases my hand, walks up to her, and kisses her cheek. "Jewels, thanks a bunch for doing this."

"Anytime." She gives him a small hug before stepping back. "Although, I'm very curious as to who the lucky woman is that all this was done for." Her gaze finds me, and she smiles. "I'm assuming this is her?"

"Yep." Wilder reaches back and pulls me to his side. "This is Zhara."

"Hmm ..." She assesses me with a curious gaze. "She's very pretty. This could actually be a lot of fun."

"What could be a lot of fun?" I ask, struggling not to fidget, but her intense assessment of me is making me nervous.

"Dressing you up." Grinning, Wilder spins me around and makes me do a little twirl. "Making you all sparkly."

I laugh as he spins me to a stop, then grip onto his arm as dizziness overtakes me.

"Hmm ... I'll be right back." Jewels ambles back through the doorway that she entered from.

"We should eat while we wait for her," Wilder suggests, slipping his arm around my lower back. "She might be a while."

Nodding, Jett launches himself over the back of the sofa

and sinks down onto the cushions. "I'm so freakin' starving." He grabs a plate and starts loading waffles onto it.

"Me, too." Jackson winds around and sits down beside Jett. "You know, we always give Ridge crap about not taking care of himself, but I think we all forget to eat sometimes."

"We're all good at remembering to shower, though." Wilder plops down onto the sofa, and I take a seat next to him. "Ridge is the only one that has a problem with that."

"For sure," Jett says around a mouthful of waffles.

Jackson frowns at Jett. "You didn't even put any syrup on it."

Jett stuffs another bite of waffles into his mouth. "That's because I don't like it."

Jackson lifts a brow at him. "Since when?"

Jett gives a half-shrug. "Since forever."

Jackson's brows dip as he picks up a plate. "Huh? You learn something new every day." He places a couple of waffles onto a plate then collects the bottle of syrup, glancing at me. "What about you, cute girl? Are you a syrup lover like Wilder and I, or a syrup hater like this crazy asshole?" He gives a not-so-discreet nod at Jett while grinning.

Jett doesn't seem to mind, completely engulfed in stuffing waffles into his mouth.

"I love syrup." I take the plate that Wilder hands to me. "My dad used to make it from scratch, and it was so good. My mom tried to make it once, but she sucked at cooking."

It's weird to be talking about my parents like this, a simple memory that has nothing to do with lies and secrets. It does make me think of that stupid hologram, though, and my heart aches a little.

It wasn't real.

My mom is still dead.

"I'm not a very good cook either," I admit as I pick up a fork and put a couple of waffles onto my plate. "My sister Jessamine, though, is living in London right now so she can attend this fancy culinary school."

"That's cool," Jackson says as he pours syrup onto his waffles. "I can't cook for shit, either. Neither can Jett or Xavier. Ridge is okay, and so is Benton."

"But I am the best," Wilder states with a proud grin. Then he sits back in the sofa and balances his plate on his lap. "When things settle down a bit, I'll have to cook something for you."

"Like a dinner?" I ask. "Or do you bake?"

"Is there a difference?" Jackson wonders as stuffs a bite of waffles into his mouth.

"Dude, there's a huge difference," Wilder tells him, wiping some syrup off his fingers with a napkin. "Dinners require sautéing, chopping, seasoning—stuff like that. Baking is all sugar and ovens, like cookies and brownies."

"And cakes," I add. "Man, I haven't had a homemade cake since Jessa left," I say the latter more to myself as I take a bite of the waffles.

It feels weird talking about my family when I'm not certain if they know about me, where I come from, that I may have been adopted.

How much do any of them know about this? Will I ever get the chance to ask?

"I can make you one," Wilder offers, chucking the napkin onto the table. "I love making cakes."

"Since when?" Jackson questions with a cock of his brow.

Wilder shrugs. "Since forever."

"Or since now?" Speculation floods Jackson's tone.

Wilder gives him a dirty look, and Jackson gives him the same look back.

Um ... My gaze dance between the two of them, puzzlement twirling through me.

And things only get more confusing when Jackson stands up.

"Hey, I need to talk to you for a second," he tells Wilder, slanting forward to set his plate down on the table.

Wilder rolls his eyes but places his plate on the table, stands up, and then follows Jackson across the store and back out the entrance door.

I glance at Jett. "Is everything okay with them?"

"Hmm ..." he mumbles. "I'm sure it will be after they hash this out."

My gaze flicks from the entrance door back to Jett. "Hash what out?"

Jett wavers then puts the plate down and rotates in the chair to face me. "Let's just say that they're having a conflicting problem of the same interest."

I blink. "What?"

He chuckles, scratching the side of his cheek. "Yeah, that made more sense in my head. But it sounded weird out loud." He rubs his scruffy jawline. "Hmmm... I guess the easiest way to say it is they're having a bro fight."

"Over what?"

"Um... Waffles?" he says it more like a question. "And whether or not they should both be putting syrup on them."

I still have no clue what he's talking about, but Jewels walks back into the room and ends the conversation.

EIGHTEEN

PRETTY DRESSES AND A LOT OF STARING

JEWELS HAS a dress she wants me to try on, along with a couple of outfits that I'm supposed to wear until I can get to my house and get some of my own clothes.

"Try on the dress first," Jewels tells me before ushering me into a dressing room.

She hangs all the outfits and black dress on a hook on the door then walks out, shutting the door behind her.

I eyeball the black dress she told me to put on first. It's long-sleeved and floor-length, so it doesn't seem that bad at first. But then I notice the slit running all the way up the side and the top section is made of lace, half see-through, except for in the chest area. And the top part of the back is all the way open.

"How am I supposed to even wear a bra with this?" I whisper, shaking my head.

As if sensing I was going to think that, Jewels reaches over the top of the dressing room with a backless, strapless bra in her hand. "Put this on. We'll figure out the right kind of under-wear once we're sure this is the dress."

"Make sure to model those, too," I hear Jackson say.

It's followed by chuckling, and my cheeks warm.

But, despite my embarrassment, I'm glad it sounds like they're over their bro fight. Of course, this isn't going to make trying on clothes and apparently modeling for them any easier. Part of me wants to say *no*, wants to refuse to model the clothes. But I remind myself that I agreed to do this, to work undercover for them, to help them out. And wearing this dress is part of that, part of the role I agreed to play. And, while I could stand here and convince myself that I could just quit, I'm not sure I can. Not with everything that's been going on. I need them. I can admit that.

What's harder to admit, though, is that part of me doesn't want to quit. Wants to stay in this world and play this new role that I'm slowly creating.

It's scary to think about, so I shove the thought away and focus on not thinking about it right now.

Taking a deep breath, I strip off my clothes, put on the backless, strapless bra, and then step into the dress, pulling it up over my hips and slipping my arms through the sleeves. Once I get it on, I reach back to zip up the lower section, but the zipper is stuck.

Great. I think I'm going to need some help.

"Um, Jewels? Guys?" I call out. "I need some help zipping this dress up. Can you send Jewels in here?"

"She ran over to the restaurant a few buildings down to help the owner with something," Wilder replies then someone taps on the door. "I can do it for you."

I bite my bottom lip. "Maybe I should just wait for Jewels to come back."

"She might be a bit, and we're running low on time," he says. "I promise you can trust me with this."

Can I? I barely know him. And I'm not the sort of girl who would let a guy zip up her dress. At least I used to not be. But so much has happened and, honestly, after the crappy day I had, Wilder was the one who briefly took my mind off what happened when we sang together.

Crossing one arm over my chest to hold the dress in place, I reach for the door handle and crack open the door. "Okay, you can come in."

He squeezes inside with a glass of orange juice in his hand, shuts the door, then turns around, and then scrolls his gaze up and down me. "Holy crap, you look ..." He shakes his head, his wide eyes full of awe. "Fucking beautiful." His gaze welds with mine. "I wanted to think of a more poetic word, but I think I'm a little tired or something. Seriously, though ..." He intensely looks me over again. "You look perfectly and utterly gorgeous."

Heat spreads to every single part of my flesh. "Thanks."

He presses back an amused smile. "You're welcome."

Silence skips by as he continues to look me over, causing my blush to increase.

"Sorry. I'll stop staring," he finally says. Then he hands me the glass of juice. "Hold this while I get the dress zipped up."

I take the glass, and he winds around me, grazing his fingers along the exposed skin of my lower back as he bunches up the dress to pull up the zipper.

"Shit, this thing is stuck," he murmurs, his knuckles continuously brushing against my skin as he struggles to get the zipper to go up. "Is it ...? Okay ... There we go—"

Zip.

The zipper goes up, and then his fingers leave my back.

A shaky exhale fumbles from my lips, and I realize I'd been holding my breath.

"Hopefully, it won't be as much of a pain in the ass when we have to take it off," he remarks then a drop of silence trickles by. "Can I try something?"

I swallow hard as I nod, uncertain why I'm even nervous.

"I just want to put your hair up for a second," he adds, moving around in front of me.

"I don't have a hair elastic," I inform him, my heart speeding up as his eyes scroll over me again.

"That's okay. I always have one on me." Winking, he removes a hair elastic from his wrist. I must give him a perplexed look, because he smiles and says, "Hey, I sometimes like to pull my hair out of my face." He reaches for my hair. "While I love my longer hair, it can get in the way, like while I'm painting."

"I can see that." I reach up and brush strands of his hair out of his face. I don't even know why I do it. It just sort of happens.

His brows furrow as he tilts his head to the side, but he doesn't comment on my weird move—thankfully—rolling his tongue in his mouth then focusing on pulling my hair up.

Between my embarrassing move and how ... warm my body feels as he moves his fingers through my hair, I can barely get any oxygen into my lungs. And my heart is an erratic mess inside my chest, pounding so hard, and my throat is as dry as sandpaper.

Why am I so nervous?

Better yet, why do I get this way around guys?

Why can't I be more like Taylor? Confident.

Sucking in an unsteady breath, I absentmindedly take a long gulp of the drink that I'm holding. Only to realize it's not my drink, mostly because the weird taste draws me out of my daze.

"Crap, I'm sorry," I tell Wilder when he gives me a funny look. "I forgot this was your drink."

"It's fine. You can drink it if you want." He sucks on his lip ring. "Although, I should probably warn you that it's a mimosa."

Well, that explains the weird taste. Not that it was awful.

"I wondered why it didn't taste like orange juice."

"Yeah, it's definitely a little different. But I like it," he says as he pulls my hair up onto my head. "There's more out there, so if you want, you can drink mine."

I warily glance down at the glass in my hand. "But it has alcohol in it, right?"

"A little bit, but not a ton." He wraps the elastic around my hair. "You don't have to if you don't want to. No one's going to care if you don't drink."

I appreciate him saying that, considering how many times Taylor told me the opposite, and I have no plans on drinking it. But then he steps back and starts intensely studying me again, and I find myself taking a couple more swallows.

"Have you ever drank before?" he asks as I hand the mostly empty glass back to him.

I nod. "Once. It was actually the night I met Benton."

"What did you drink then?"

"A shot of something with Taylor, and then Benton made me a drink at the party. But he said he didn't put too much alcohol in it. I barely got to take a couple of sips before a girl bumped into me and I spilled it all over myself."

"Did she bump into you on purpose?"

I shrug, smoothing invisible creases off the front of the dress. "A lot of people that were at the party didn't want me there, because they thought I would narc on them. I guess I can't really blame them. I'm sure I seem like the kind of person that would."

"Well, people suck." He traces a path down the side of my face with his fingertip, drawing my attention to him. "Don't ever let anyone change your view of yourself in a negative manner, okay?"

I smile at him. "Okay."

He mirrors my smile. "But changing it in a positive manner is okay. Remember that, especially right now."

"Why?"

"Because I'm about to tell you something, and I want you to know that it's true."

I anxiously sink my teeth into my bottom lip. "Okay."

"Always so nervous," he remarks while messing around with my hair.

He pulls a few wisps out to frame my face then steps back and assesses me. "You are insanely gorgeous. I mean, I've always sort of noticed it from afar, but this ..." He bites down on his bottom lip as his gaze lazily skims up and down. "This goes behind beautiful."

I shift my weight, feeling super awkward. "I don't think—"

He places a finger against my lips, the corners of his lips quirking. "Shh ... Just let me admire my work of art here." He angles his head to the side and rubs his chin. I notice he has several rings on his fingers. "Yeah, I definitely picked the right dress."

"*You* picked the dress?" I can't conceal my shock.

"I'm going to not take your shock personally," he teases as he circles me. "I have an eye for these things and, while I haven't really seen you wear too much black, I had a feeling the color would look amazing on you. And I was right."

He has to be the only person to ever think that since most people tell me I seem like a pink and frilly sort of girl. I kind of like that he does see me differently.

I run my fingers over the lacy fabric of the dress. "When did you pick the dress out?"

"I looked on the store's website on our way over here and texted Jewels to get it ready. Personally, I would've preferred more time to think it over, but we're on a ticking clock. It's okay, though. I'm not even sure I could've picked a better dress for you."

"It's really pretty," I tell him. "And fancy, even more so than dresses girls wear to prom. Not that I ever went to prom, but I saw what Taylor wore."

"I didn't go to prom either. Not that I didn't want to. We were just too busy with our job." He pauses, musing over something. "If there's dancing at the ball tonight, we should dance."

Even though that sounds way out of my element, I nod. "Okay." And besides, I sexy danced for Jett so I'm sure I can figure out dancing with Wilder.

"Awesome" He smiles then grazes his fingers along the back of my neck, causing a shiver to roll through my body. "Okay, so while I love your long, wavy hair, I want you to wear your hair up like this tonight."

"I can do that."

"Good." He moves back around me and grins, his piercings glinting in the low lighting. "Okay, so are you ready to let me show you off?"

"*What ...?* To who?"

He hitches his thumb over his shoulder, pointing toward the door. "To the other members of your team."

My team?

It still sounds so weird.

I frantically shake my head. "Can't I just wait until I have to wear it to the masquerade?"

"You could, but I think they should see you beforehand. Besides, I want to show you off."

I try my best not to frown. "I guess I can show them, then." But the idea of walking out there in this dress and having Jett and Jackson stare at me ... It was uncomfortable enough with Wilder doing it. I'm not even certain why, other than I'm not used to so much attention.

Taylor was always the one getting stared at. I was just the girl who blended in with the background, and I think I was okay with that. Still am. Sure, I've wanted to change my image, but I'm unsure if I'll ever be the sort of girl who desires to be the center of attention.

He extends his hand to me. "You ready?"

Am I?

This isn't a big deal, Zhara. You've dealt with way, way worse than this.

And yet, somehow, it takes a lot of effort to place my hand in Wilder's.

"I guess so." I gather the front of the dress into my hand so I can walk.

Speaking of which...

"What shoes am I supposed to wear with this?" I ask as Wilder opens the dressing room door.

"I have a few ideas, but I'll have to have you try them all on before I decide." He casts a glance over his shoulder at me. "Please tell me you can walk in heels."

"I actually can," I assure him.

A smile lights up his face. "You're going to look epic tonight."

While part of me is excited, the other part is very aware that tonight could be dangerous. I try not to focus on that now, knowing I'll probably stress myself out if I do.

"We do need to stop by another store to grab a mask for you," Wilder tells me as he steps out of the dressing room.

"For what?"

"For the masquerade ball."

"Right. I didn't even think about that."

"It's okay. Really, we just want you to focus on staying safe, which we will be doing everything in our power to keep you that way."

My dress swishes as I exit the dressing room behind him. "I know you guys said that I'm not going to have to talk to Drake, but what if things don't work out that way? What if I have to talk to him? What am I supposed to say?"

"Benton will talk to you more about that soon." He turns to face me and positions himself in front of me so Jackson and Jett can't see me. I can hear them chatting in the background about cars, though. "In fact, he's on his way here now to talk to us. For now, I want you to soak this in."

"Soak what in?" I wonder confusedly.

A slow grin spreads across his face. "You'll see." Then he

spins back around and clears his throat. "Gentlemen, may I present to you, Zhara Baker, the girl who's going to be the most beautiful attendee at this party." He steps to the side and gives a dramatic gesture at me.

I'd probably laugh except Jackson and Jett are staring at me the same way Wilder stared at me when he first walked into the dressing room. Their eyes skate up and down me several times before either of them speak.

"Shit, dude," Jett mutters, blinking his bloodshot eyes a few times. "You did good. Like really, really good." He looks me over again then leans back in the sofa with his arms draped across the back. "She's like a work of art."

"She definitely is," Wilder agrees then looks at Jackson with his arms crossed. "So?"

Jackson leans forward, picks up a glass of mimosa, and takes a slow drink, his gaze dissecting me. Then he gradually sits back in the chair and puts his foot on his knee. "She's gorgeous." He looks at me when he says it, yet he's speaking to Wilder.

I wish he'd shift his attention to him, because his intense gaze is making my heart sprint inside my chest and a flush breaks out across my skin.

"She's more than gorgeous." Wilder glances at me, grinning. "She's perfect."

"I'm not perfect," I insist, extremely uncomfortable.

"In that dress, you fucking are," he quips, turning back to face me. "And tonight, you're going to have to be on that page, because this place that we're going to ..." He wavers. "You need to be a confident beotch."

I crinkle my nose. "I'm not sure I can do that."

He meticulously lifts his pierced brow. "There's video

footage of a couple of kisses that happened in the parking lot of Benton's apartment that suggest otherwise."

And yep, there goes my embarrassment again.

"I wasn't really being a beotch," I mutter mortified. "I was just ... being a bad girl."

"Just how I taught her," Jett muses then takes a swig of the mimosa.

"Yeah, because you're an expert on being a beotch." Wilder smirks at him.

Jett gives a blasé shrug, tucking his hands behind his head. "Yep, sure am."

I find his remark funny since, out of all the guys, Jett seems the most chill and least beotch-y.

Shaking his head, Wilder fixes his attention back on Jackson. "So, I have your approval?"

Jackson observes me again then nods. "Yeah, you do."

"Awesome." Wilder rubs his hands together. "I'll go pick out her shoes, then." He strides off toward where the merchandise is located.

I find it amusing that he needed Jackson's approval on the dress. I'm assuming it's because they both dress stylish. Sure, their styles are completely different—Wilder's more edgy while Jackson's more preppy—but you can tell they both put a lot of thought into what they wear.

"You two and your clothes," Jett remarks with a shake of his head. "You're so weird."

"We're weird?" Jackson looks at him with his brow arched. "Coming from someone who I once saw eat an entire bowl of brownie batter and crackers."

"Hey, that stuff is delicious," he insists, rising to his feet. "I gotta go do something. I'll be right back." He tosses me a smile before winding around the sofa and exiting the store.

Jackson watches him walk away with a frown on his face. "He's getting worse."

"About what?"

He sighs, twisting back around. "He used to only get high like once or twice a week on our downtime. But it's getting to the point where he does it every day."

"Is that what he went to do?"

"Probably."

"Is he addicted?"

He shakes his head, leaning forward and resting his arms on his knees. "No. Or, well, he's not addicted to getting high. I think he's addicted to the feeling he gets when he's high. Or lack of feeling, anyway."

"What do you mean?"

He deliberates then pats the spot beside him. "Come sit down. Wilder could take a while picking out your shoes."

Collecting the front of the dress in my hands, I make my way over to him and carefully sit down.

Since he didn't answer my question right away, I assume he won't. And I'm not surprised. The guys have all been pretty vague about telling me about each other's pasts.

But then Jackson says, "You know a little bit about Jett's past, right? I think he mentioned he told you some things."

"You mean about how he grew up in foster homes?" I say, recalling the brief bit of information Jett told me about him. He also said that he was going to tell me one thing about him every time we hung out, but he hasn't done that yet. Part of me wonders if he even remembers telling me that since I'm pretty sure he was blazed when he said it. Then again, we haven't spent much time together since then and no one-on-one time.

"Yeah." He stares down at his hands, momentarily growing quiet. "We all made this pact a while ago that we wouldn't talk about each other's past, so I don't want to say much more than that. It can be dangerous in our line of work for too many people to know who we really are. Not that I don't trust you. It just needs to be Jett's choice to tell you."

"That makes sense." I rest my hands on my lap. "Benton told me I should avoid telling people who I am. But Tank and Ralpho already knew somehow."

"I heard about that." He rotates toward me. "You should be okay. I mean, they won't be able to find out about your past."

"You mean that I may have been in an experimental drug facility?" I ask quietly.

He nods. "Those files are locked, and only the best hackers and people with access to them can see them. And only very high up people in the program have that access."

I can't help thinking about the time a rogue broke into Benton's apartment and how he implied that their bosses didn't tell the guys everything. Not that I believe the rogue, but I also don't know very much about the program. And who is their boss even? He's supposed to be paying them a visit. I wonder if I'll meet him.

Wait. Does the program even know I'm involved in this case?

"How did you guys find out what was in my files?" I wonder. "Or do you have access?"

Jackson lets out a soft laugh as he shakes his head. "Nah, it takes years and years of working your way up into the program to gain access to that. We do, however, have one of the best hackers on our team."

I frown, remembering how Benton told me Ridge was going to hack into some files to find out about my family's past. "So, those were the files Ridge was hacking into?" I ask, and he nods. "Aren't you guys worried he's going to get in trouble if he gets caught?"

"He won't get caught," he assures me. "Ridge has been doing stuff like this for years."

"But he's only eighteen."

"I know. But the guy is super smart."

"He is." I know for a fact that he is, since he was in most of my honors classes.

"From what I hear, you are, too."

A touchy subject for me. "I wouldn't say super smart, but I didn't put a lot of time and focus into school. I'm actually supposed to be starting summer classes for college, but I decided to do this instead."

"Really?" he says. "Can I ask why?"

"Because it was different, and I wanted different," I admit, tracing the patterns of the lace on the dress with my fingertip. "Is that weird?"

"Not at all." He considers something. "Do you regret your choice?"

I think about it for a moment then shake my head. "I don't think I do."

"Even after everything that's happened?"

"I think so."

"Good." He smiles almost in relief. "In order to survive in this world, you have to be okay with learning dark things, not just about others but about yourself. The fact that you haven't freaked out yet probably means you'll be okay to continue playing your role in all this."

"You mean Benton's fake girlfriend?"

He hesitates then nods. "You can have other roles, too. You don't just have to be Benton's girlfriend. And when you're just hanging out with us and are not undercover, you can be yourself."

"Do you guys get time to just hang out? Because it kind of seems like you don't."

"These last few weeks have been sort of hectic, but it's not always this crazy." He brushes strands of my hair out of my face. "And we're kind of hanging out now."

"I guess we kind of are."

"You sound doubtful."

"I'm not doubtful. I just ... haven't spent much time with guys or friends in general, so I'm not sure if hanging out and trying on clothes is a normal thing to do while hanging out." As soon as the words leave my lips, I mentally roll my eyes at myself. "Oh my gosh, I probably sound so lame."

His lips quirk in amusement. "No, you sound adorable." He scoots toward me. "And to answer your questions, yes, there've been times where I've spent time hanging out with friends and trying on clothes. Although, that's usually just with Wilder. None of the other guys really give a shit about what they wear, which is probably pretty obvious," he jokes with a grin. "Although, we've never took a girl shopping."

"Seriously?"

"Yeah. But again, why the doubt?"

"I don't know ... You've hung out with a lot of girls, so it seems like you would've at least taken one of them with you."

His brow teases upward. "How do you know I've hung out with a lot of girls?"

"I ..." You just what? Watched him from afar, like you sometimes did with all the other bad boy rebels? Wow, I'm really on a spazz roll, aren't I? "I've just seen you hanging out with girls sometimes."

He rolls his tongue in his mouth, biting back a smile. "That's because I'm a notorious flirt. But I think you probably already know that."

I lift my shoulders, shrugging. "I guess so."

Amusement sparkles in his eyes. "I think you know so. But, I guess, since you're not sure, I'll have to show you." Then he scoots closer to me, tracing the pad of his thumb along my bottom lip, a slight smile playing at the corners of his lips. "Yep, they look as soft as I expected. Maybe even softer."

"I ..." I have no clue what to say. I've never actually flirted before, and I'm not even sure if he wants me to flirt back.

He chuckles at my sputtering and blushing, but then he grows serious. He subtly glances over his shoulder to where Wilder is busy looking through shoes. Then his attention returns to me. "I know you don't like hearing this, but I'm going to say it anyway. You're ridiculously cute, and if it weren't for some certain conflicting issues, I'd totally fucking kiss you right now."

"As part of the job?" I stammer. Because seriously, what the crap? No, there's no way... It has to be because of the job...

He shakes his head. "No, we're hanging out right now, remember?"

I nod like I understand, but I'm completely perplexed.

Is he saying he wants to kiss me just to kiss me?

Before I can even attempt to answer that question, the bell on the front door dings and Benton and Xavier walk in.

When Jackson spots them, he casually lowers his finger from my lips and scoots over a little bit.

"Hey." Jackson greets them with a quizzical knit at his brow. "I thought we were meeting at your place ... And aren't you supposed to be getting answers out of Charles?"

As they get closer, I note how stressed out they both look.

Jackson must notice it, too, because he heaves out a weighted sigh. "What the hell happened now?"

They stop beside the sofa, Benton fixing his attention on Jackson while Xavier gives me a subtle once-over. Unlike everyone else, he seems indifferent to my makeover.

"The boss showed up and took him into custody," Benton explains with a trace of annoyance.

"What?" Jackson gapes at him. "Why the hell for?"

"He said it was for safety reasons and that the program has been trying to get ahold of Charles for quite a while." The muscle in his jaw spasms. "It's frustrating, though, because he may have had answers to why rogues are tormenting Zhara."

"Can't you just interrogate him while he's in custody?" Jackson asks. "That should be allowed."

"Usually, it is. But, apparently, there's something in Charles's file that prohibits us from doing so," Benton explains, sitting down on the back of the sofa. "But the boss wouldn't specify what."

Jackson's lips curve downward. "Well, that's shitty news."

"It gets worse." Xavier sits on the back of the sofa beside Benton. "Because the boss is on his way over here right now to talk to Zhara. He'll be here in like fifteen to twenty minutes."

"What?" I whisper at the same time Jackson says, "What the hell? How did he even find out about her?"

"Someone reported it to him, but he didn't specify who," Benton replies, opening and flexing his hands. "I'm annoyed as hell. I didn't want him finding out about her."

"Why?" I utter quietly, drawing all their attentions to me.

Benton's expression softens when his gaze meets mine. "A few reasons, but the biggest one is that I didn't want them finding out about your past. Or, well, at least until we looked into more."

"It's too late for that now," Xavier mutters. "And now she's going to have to talk to him, and you haven't even prepared her for it. And if she says the wrong thing, we could end up screwed."

"Oh, shut the fuck up, Xav." Wilder strolls over from the shoe racks with two pairs of heels in his hands. "Zhara can handle this as long as you don't put doubt in her head." He stops beside the sofa, sets the shoes down on the table, and then holds out his hand to me. "But first, we've gotta get you out of this dress and into a more appropriate outfit."

I wonder what qualifies as an appropriate outfit as I place my hand in his and let him help me to my feet. He keeps ahold of my hand as we make our way back to the dressing room.

When we reach the door, he opens it and ushers me inside.

"Wait ..." Benton stiffens as he watches us walk away. "Why the hell are you going in with her while she changes?"

"Because I have to help her get out of the dress," Wilder replies like it's so obvious. Then he steps inside the dressing room with me, shuts the door, and swings around behind me.

Like when he put it on, his knuckles brush against the small of my back as he unzips the dress.

Knock, knock, knock.

"Wilder," Benton says from the other side of the door, "I don't think it's really appropriate for you to be in there while she's changing."

Wilder chuckles under his breath. "I think our stern leader might be a little bit jealous, princess."

Jealous? Why? "We should probably tell him that I'm not changing."

"Now, what would be the fun in that?" he remarks amusedly.

"Is it fun not to tell him?" I wonder confusedly.

"Abso-fucking-lutely. Because Benton getting all wound up can be funny as hell." He releases a quiet sigh. "However, now's probably not the best time. Not with him so stressed out with you meeting the boss."

I gulp. "Is it ...? Is it going to be bad?"

"No ... The boss ... He can just be intense sometimes. And intimidating." He steps back from me. "Plus, there's stuff we don't want him knowing yet about the case. We were going to prep you about that stuff before you ever met him. And we can still do that. It's just a little bit nerve-racking when we only have a handful of minutes."

Worry stirs through me. "What if I mess up and say the wrong thing?"

He steps around in front of me. "You won't."

"How can you be so sure?"

"Because you've already handled a lot of intense situations without any preparing." He angles his head to the side and glances over me while tapping his lip "Now, I just need to figure out what the hell to put you in while you meet the boss."

"Wilder." Benton knocks on the door again.

"Dude, chill out," Wilder says with an eye roll. "I just unzipped her dress for her, and now I'm figuring out what she should put on. I'll step out when she changes."

"Okay." Silence trickles by. "Sweetheart, I don't want to rush you, but please get changed as quickly as you can so I can talk to you about a few things."

"Okay," I tell him while Wilder gives me a curious look.

"When did he start calling you sweetheart?" He sifts through the clothes that Jewels stuck in here earlier.

I shrug. "I'm not sure. Why?"

He lifts a shoulder. "Just curious." He reaches for the door handle. "I need to go grab a different outfit. I'll be right back." He hurries out and closes the door behind him.

Silence immediately enfolds around me, along with tension.

I can't shake the feeling that the guys are worried about me meeting their boss.

No, not worried.

Scared.

Why?

What could they be so afraid of?

NINETEEN

CITRUS, RAIN, AND A THREAT

WHEN WILDER RETURNS, he has a button shirt with a bow on the collar, a pleated skirt, knee-high stockings, and heeled back shoes. It's a very business-like outfit, and while it leans more toward my old style, it's still more nice than anything I've ever worn.

"The boss likes us to look put-together whenever he has a meeting with us," Wilder explains as he hands me the outfit. "I'm assuming it'll be the same for you."

Nervousness swells inside me as I take the clothes from him, and I part my lips with questions, but he's already rushing out the door.

Exhaling shakily, I step out of the dress and start putting on the outfit.

"So, I'm not sure what he's going to ask you," Benton suddenly says from the other side of the door, "or how he even found out about you, but I want to go over a couple of things instead of just throwing you in there blind."

"Okay." My fingers shake as I do up the buttons on the shirt.

"Try to keep your answers as vague as possible," he starts. "We usually don't give him complete details on what we've been up to, to avoid him trying to take over the case. I also want you to try not to mention anything about Alexis. I don't know if he's aware yet if she's with another group. It's also good if you look him directly in the eye while talking to him, even though you may not want to."

"Why would I not want to?" I ask as I slip the skirt on then sit down on the bench in the dressing room to put the knee-high stockings on.

"Because his face is a little ... startling," he tells me with hesitancy. "A long time ago, he was involved in a case where a drug lord found out about him and punished his face with a knife. He could've had some surgeries to fix the scarring, but he refused; said he wanted to have a reminder of the pain."

I gulp down a shaky breath. "Okay. So, be vague, don't mention Alexis, and look him in the eye ... Is there anything else?"

"Just try not to be nervous." He grows quiet for a moment. "Are you dressed yet?"

"Yeah, I'm just putting my shoes on."

"Can I come in?"

I glance at the door, noting I forgot to lock it. "Sure."

A second later, the door is opened, and he steps in, shutting the door behind him.

His gaze quickly roams over me. "Wilder picked a good outfit," he states, extending his hand to me to help me up.

I slip on the heels then place my hand in his. Then he pulls me to my feet.

"You'll be okay," he tells me, grazing his knuckles along my jawline. "You've handled a lot worse."

I feel like he's trying to reassure himself, and that only makes me more nervous.

"And keep your phone on you no matter what." He pauses then leans forward and brushes his lips across mine.

I give a nervous nod, stuffing my phone into the pocket of my shirt, confusion spinning through me. He's kissed me a few times behind closed doors and I'm starting to get confused about it. Why does he want to pretend like we're girlfriend and boyfriend even when no one else is around?

Not that I dare ask him.

I remain quiet as we exit the dressing room and head toward the entrance doors. The rest of the guys offer me encouraging smiles, but nervousness resides in their eyes.

"Where am I supposed to meet him?" I ask as Benton pushes open the door.

He points to a black car parked near the store. The windows are tinted so much that I can't see inside it, and everything about it reminds me of Axel.

An uneven breath fumbles from my lips, and Benton gives my hand a squeeze.

"Relax," he tries to encourage as he leads me toward the car. Then he opens the back door and gestures for me to get in.

I take one last glance at him before lowering my head and ducking inside.

The first thing I notice as I slide onto the seat is the familiarity of the scent in the air—citrusy mixed with the aroma of rain. The smell makes blurry images flicker through my mind, but none of them make any sense. My stomach churns for some reason, though, and for a moment, I worry I might vomit.

But I swallow the feeling down and focus on the man sitting in the seat across from mine.

He's about in his mid-forties with short, brown hair and is wearing a suit and tie. He also has elevated scars on his face; vertical lines that run down his cheek. Instead of staring at those, I carry his gaze.

"Zhara Baker, I presume?" he asks, and I nod. "I've learned a lot about you over the last couple of hours. Unfortunately, there's still a lot to learn about you." He crosses his arms, keeping his gaze trained on me. "Because, for some strange reason, most of your files have been erased." His gaze burrows into me. "Do you have any idea why?"

I promptly shake my head. "No."

"Hmm ... I find it interesting that you say you know nothing about it, yet you appear out of nowhere, invading one of my teams and their cases."

Remembering what Benton said, I make certain to be vague. "I didn't invade the team or case."

"Didn't you?" he questions.

I shake my head. "No."

He hesitates momentarily. "You're aware of your background, correct?" he asks, and I nod. "And I'm sure you're aware that it's causing quite the problem for my team."

I want to shake my head, but he's kind of right, so I give a small nod.

"Well, at least you're honest," he says. "But that still doesn't help the problem of rogues navigating toward you, which means they navigate toward my team. And if it weren't for Drake requesting a meeting with you, I'd remove you from the team immediately. But, unfortunately, doing so right now would compromise a huge chance to move forward with this case. So, for now, I'll let you continue to be part of the team. However, I will be looking into your background more, and I will get to the bottom of why these rogues are after you." He slants forward, his eyes darkening. "And if I find out that you're doing anything sneaky that could compromise this, there will be consequences, understand?"

I give an unsteady nod, my palms grossly sweaty, but I resist the urge to wipe them off, not wanting to reveal how nervous I am.

"Good." He reclines back in the seat. "You can go now. I'll be in touch."

More than eager to get the hell out of the car, I grab the door handle, shove the door open, and then jump out of the car. None of the guys are waiting in the parking lot for me, so I powerwalk back to the store while the boss drives away.

Inside the store, I find the guys lounging around on the sofas, looking extremely uneasy. Jett is there too. He must've come in while I was in the car.

They all visibly relax when they see me.

"What'd he want?" Wilder sets down the glass that he's holding and rotates around in the sofa to look at me.

I glance at the four of them and shrug. "Nothing really. He just wanted to make sure that I understood he was going to look into my background and why the rogues were after me. He also wanted to make sure I wouldn't do anything to compromise the case."

"Did he threaten you?" Benton asks, tension rippling off of him.

I shake my head, but he reads right through my lie.

"He did, didn't he?" he presses.

I sigh, making my way over to the sofa and sitting down

between Benton and Jackson. "It wasn't really a threat. It was more like a warning."

Jackson grinds his teeth from side to side. "Why does he always gotta be a dick?"

"He's just trying to make sure we're safe." Jett rubs his blood shot eyes with the heels of his hands. "But yeah, I wish he'd be less of a dick about it."

"I know," Wilder agrees, rising to his feet and stretching his arms above his head. His shirt rides up slightly and again, I catch sight of his cars. "But, at least we got that out of the way and now we can focus on more important stuff. Like getting you ready for the ball." He lowers his hands to his sides.

"You mean, I have to get in the dress again?" I ask, and Wilder nods. "But I just got out of it." I try not to pout, but it was such a pain getting into it.

"Yep, but the masquerade starts in like three hours, and we still have to do your makeup, shoes, and accessories," he explains. "Plus, I want to work on your hair a bit."

Sighing quietly, I get to my feet and start to follow Wilder back to the dressing room.

"Zhara," Benton calls out before I step inside.

I turn around. "Yeah?"

Uncertainty fills his expression as he rises to his feet and takes a few steps toward me, lowering his voice. "Did the boss say anything else to you?"

I shake my head. "Not really ... One thing that was kind of weird, though, is when I got in the car, the smell inside of it reminded me of something. I just couldn't place what. It also made me feel kind of sick." I honestly wouldn't have said anything about it, except the last time I had that sense of famil-iarity was when I was getting in the car with Axel.

"What was the scent?" he wonders, frowning.

"Citrus mixed with rain."

He presses his lips together, indifference washing over his expression.

"Is everything okay?" I ask.

He puts on a fake smile. "Yeah."

I want to press him more, but Wilder snags ahold of my hand and pulls me into the dressing room.

The sinking feeling that Benton is keeping something from me remains inside my stomach. I just hope he's not lying to me again.

TWENTY

JACKSON

"THAT SMELL SHE RECOGNIZED," I say the moment Zhara goes into the dressing room and out of earshot. "You know what that is, right?"

Benton huffs out a frustrated exhale as he returns to the sofa and sits down. "Yeah, I fucking know what it is." He scrubs his hand across the top of his head. "I just wish I didn't."

"Yeah, me either." A chill slithers down my spine as I recall the many days I was forced to smell that scent.

The days I spent in the drug facility.

"What I don't understand is why the boss would smell like that," Benton mutters, scratching at his arm. "He didn't smell like that when I talked to him earlier."

"Maybe it was just the inside of the car that smelled like that," I suggest then take a long swig of the mimosa, knowing I'm going to need it with how stressful everything is getting. And I don't handle stress very well.

"Still, why would it smell like that in his car?" Benton shakes his head, his jaw set tight. "It doesn't make any sense."

"Unless he was seeing how Zhara would react to it," Jett chimes in, his eyes even more bloodshot than they were a half an hour ago.

He's sitting in the sofa across from me with his feet kicked up on the table, looking as relaxed as can be. At this rate, we may have to have him stay away from the ball, or he'll risk blowing our cover.

We also might have to have an intervention with him soon, but that's something I need to talk about with Benton.

"Why would he do that?" Benton says, glancing at Jett with a crease between his brow. "He already knows she's from an experimental drug facility."

"True." Jett rubs his bloodshot eyes. "I was just offering an explanation."

"Maybe he was at an experimental drug facility recently," I say, the idea making blood roar in my eardrums.

"But we haven't heard of any reports of that," Benton reminds me. "And that still wouldn't explain why his car would smell like that. It's weird, though ... and I think we need to look into it."

"Should we tell Zhara?" I ask as I set the mimosa down. "I mean, clearly the smell affected her. And I ... I don't like lying to her."

Benton gives me an insinuating look. "You don't, huh?"

I mimic his look. "You know, if you're implying something, then just say it."

"Okay." Benton reclines back in the sofa with his arms crossed. "I told everyone before I brought her into our group to not get too attached, and yet, just earlier you and Wilder were outside arguing over her."

"How did you find out about that?" I ask, trying not to

squirm. When Jett pulls a *whoops* face, I shake my head. "Never mind."

"That doesn't even matter. Just make sure to stay just friends with her, okay?" Benton stands up and wanders toward the dressing room door.

"Does that go for you, too?" I call after him.

Tension waves in his body as he gradually turns toward me. "I don't need to be reminded. I have no problem with staying just friends with her."

"Sure you do," I disagree with him, but let the subject drop.

Deep down, I know Benton is right. That we all need to stay friends with her, or there will be a lot of problems amongst the group.

The problem is that I feel connected to Zhara in a way I've never felt before. But that's probably because of our pasts. At least, that's what I'm telling myself for now. Part of me knows I'm lying, though.

AS I'M WAITING for Zhara to get dressed in her dress—that damn dress that she looks unbelievably gorgeous in—I get a call from Ridge. Since the store owner has returned to the store, I wander outside to take the call.

"Please tell me you got some sort of answers," I answer as I lean against the side of the brick building. "Because without Charles, we're back to square one unless you can trace the hologram."

"I didn't exactly trace it." The hesitancy and worry in his tone instantly puts me on edge. "However, during my search, it led me to a website where people were talking about these hologram devices. It was total dark web shit, and I was going to get off it as soon as I realized how deep into the web I'd gotten, but then I ended up getting caught up in this chat with a group of rogues and..." Again, he hesitates, which is kind of out of character for him.

"Come on, Ridge, just spit it out," I say, losing a bit of my patience, mostly because I'm stressed out.

Not just over this thing with Zhara, but because of the boss visiting. He rarely pays unexpected visits unless he has a purpose. But the only reason he seemed to be here is to talk to Zhara and take Charles into custody—or take him away from us, depending on how I want to look at it. And his visit with Zhara lasted only a couple of minutes. I also find it strange that Zhara's description of the scent of inside of the Boss's car smelled similar to drug experimental facilities, like he was just at one. But if he was, why didn't he mention it?

It's definitely something we're going to have to look into, but we'll have to be careful about it. If we've learned one thing in this world, it's trust no one, even the boss. In fact, the only people I do trust are my team members. But they're like brothers to me.

"On this chat," Ridge says, drawing me from my thoughts. "They... they were talking about Zhara's sister Alexis and how she used to be a drug experimental subject."

"Shit," I mutter, pinching the brim of my nose, feeling a headache coming on. "Although, I'm not that surprised considering Zhara probably is from one too."

"I wasn't either," he tells me. "But what did surprise me, though, is that they were implying that the drugs being tested on Alexis while she was in an experimental facility were to make her into an... assassin."

"What?" I breathe out, straightening, panic soaring through me.

"I'm not positive if it's true," he continues. "But the rogues are planning on going after her and all the drug experimental test subjects like her, so..." He doesn't finish.

But he doesn't have to.

I get the gist of what he's saying.

I glance at the store door. I can see Zhara inside, wearing her dress, and talking to Wilder.

So beautiful.

God I can't stand how beautiful she is.

And sweet as hell.

So sweet.

How can this be true?

"There's no way," I mumble. "She's way too sweet and quiet..."

"You know that might not matter. If she ever was being trained to be one, it's been years since this all happened, and she probably doesn't even remember any of it ... From what I understand, there's a lot of brainwashing that comes with assassins. At least the ones I've done research on. And usually, there's a trigger, maybe an object, that sets them off... makes them go into assassination mode."

"What are you getting at?" I ask. "Because it feels like you're getting at something."

"Well, I just think it's a bit strange that the rogues broke into Jackson and Wilder's house, only to put a hologram of Zhara's mom in there and her mom's old necklace. It's almost like they were trying to taunt Zhara into breaking."

"Wait... Are you saying you think the necklace might be a trigger for Zhara? Or her mom? Because that's a weird as hell theory... And besides, Zhara didn't react to either of those."

"It's not as weird as you think. And she may have not reacted to them, but I think the rogues may have been testing her, seeing if she would react... Like maybe they're trying to figure out her trigger."

"But why?" I ask, still unsure if I believe his theory. Not that I've never heard weird stuff like this. I know shit like this exists. It's just crazy to think of Zhara as once being an assassin. Not to mention, if she finds out, this might break her. "If the rogues are trying to eliminate these assassins, why test her?"

"They never said they were trying to eliminate them. In fact, in the chat, they were pretty vague about their end game. But that doesn't mean I can't find out. I'm going to keep looking into this more. There's actually a couple of chat members that I might be able to find out the identities too. I can also try to track some IP address," he tells me. "I just wanted to give you a heads up about this, so you guys could keep an eye on her."

"Thanks," I tell him. "And don't push yourself too hard."

"Yeah..." he mutters distractedly over the sound a keyboard clicking. "Talk to you soon. At least, I hope it's soon." He hangs up.

I sigh, then pocket my phone and turns toward the door, watching Zhara through the glass. Wilder is playing with her hair while talking to her. I have no clue what he's saying, but whatever it is, is making her blush.

It makes me aware that even if it turns out Zhara used to be one of these assassin drug test subjects, there's no way she could be dangerous now. I want to get answers, though. For her. For us.

So we can find out the best way to protect her.

TWENTY-TWO

THE STORY OF GUILT

I'M IN MY DRESS, my hair is done up, and I'm sitting on one of the sofas in the dressing room, sipping on a mimosa, mostly because I'm stressed out and the warmth of the drink seems to be helping. I'm not sure if it's a healthy thing to do or not. Maybe not. But honestly, nothing about what's going on is probably healthy. Plus, I'm some sort of drug experimental subject so, yeah...

"How much of that have you had to drink?" Benton asks me, as he steps up beside the sofa.

He's been outside for a while, talking on the phone to someone. I'm not sure about what, but I saw him through the window, and he appeared extremely stressed out.

"Only like half a glass," I tell him, twirling the glass in my hand. "Is that okay?"

He gives a nod while his gaze briefly flicks up and down me. "Yeah. You can do whatever you want. I just know you don't really drink."

"I know. I just..." A faltering breath eases from my lips.

"I'm just kind of nervous, not just with everything going on, but with having to meet this drug lord guy, Drake." I take another sip of the mimosa. "The last time I met one—Axel well, things didn't end up very well."

"I know, but we were thrown off guard then." He sits down beside me with a weighted sigh. "We'll be more prepared this time." He restlessly bounces his leg up and down. "What I really want, though, is to find a way for you not to go at all. I've been thinking maybe we should just say you're sick or something and couldn't make it."

"Would that work?" I ask warily.

He shakes his head and shrugs. "I have no idea what would happen if we did that, but at least you wouldn't have to deal with meeting Drake, Tank, and Ralpho. I mean, we had a plan on how to make sure that didn't happen even if you went to the masquerade, but with everything going on... I'm worried our plan could go to shit."

I lick a drop of mimosa off my lip then set the glass down on the table in front of me. "If me not going will get you guys into trouble, then I'd rather go and talk to Drake. I just don't want to mess up anything or say the wrong thing."

"If it did end up that you had to talk to him, we'd make you wear an earpiece," he informs me, twisting to face me. "But I refuse to let you have a meeting with him alone, which I know is going to be an issue."

"Can't you just tell him you're nervous about letting me talk to him by myself? I'm supposed to be your girlfriend, so it seems reasonable for you to request that I don't meet him by myself."

"It does. However, people like Drake that are higher up are used to getting what they want whenever they want it. But maybe if I pushed it, he might be willing to let me go with you." He contemplates something, worrying his bottom lip between his teeth. "I need to talk to the guys..." He yanks himself from his daze and his gaze scans the store; the shoe area, the racks, and then the dressing room. "Where is everyone anyway?"

I point at the dressing room doors. "They're getting dressed."

"Right." He straightens, rubbing his hand over his head. "I should probably get ready too." He lowers his hand, looking at me. "Which one is Wilder in? I need to find out what the hell he wants me to wear to this thing."

So I'm not the only one Wilder picks out outfits for? I wonder if he picked out all the guy's outfits. They had all gone back into the back section of the store to grab their attire, so I'm not sure.

And what about Ridge? He isn't here? Is he even going?

"He's on the second one from the right," I tell Benton, and he nods, getting up and striding off toward the dressing rooms.

He knocks on the dressing room door that Wilder is in then opens it up and steps inside.

As silence wraps around me, I sit back in the sofa and cross my legs.

Wilder hasn't given me any shoes to wear yet, so my feet are bare. My toenails are painted from a pedicure Taylor and I got a couple of weeks ago. I chose pink, a color I usually always choose. And normally, it goes with my outfits, but right now, with the black dress I'm wearing, it seems too bright almost.

Maybe I should paint them black. Not now, of course, but later, after the party.

But what's even going to happen after the party?

That thought makes me realize just how little I know about my future. Me, Zhara Baker, has no clue what's going to happen tomorrow.

Nervousness startles to bubble inside my stomach and my lungs suddenly feel very tight.

Panic.

I'm about to have a panic attack.

I need some fresh air.

Gathering the front of the dress in my hand, I stand up and hurry toward the front door. The fabric of the dress rustles as I step outside, a light warm summer breeze dancing around me.

Breathe, Zhara. Air in. Air out.

I take a few deep breaths. Then a couple of others. And slowly, the oxygen returns to my lungs. Not all the way, though, pressure still lingering in my chest, and I find myself wishing that Jackson had already taught me those breathing exercises.

I'm about to turn around and go inside when I notice a trail of smoke snaking out from a narrow alleyway between the store and the restaurant beside it. The scent reminds me of what the garage used to smell like every time Loki hung out in there during his high school days. While Jett had gone into the back section of the store with Wilder, Jackson, and Xavier, I'd never seen he walk out.

Did he exit out the back doors of the store so he could smoke?

Does it really matter?

I move to head back inside, but a strange pull tugs at my chest. I'm not certain what's causing it, but I turn the other way and pad toward the alleyway. When I peer around the corner, Jett is crouched down in the shadows with his head lowered in his hands, a joint between his fingers and smoke lacing the air.

He's the portrait of pain and misery and it tugs at my heart. Before I can even comprehend what I'm doing, I step into the alleyway.

"Jett?" I say as I approach him cautiously.

His head snaps up, his bloodshot eyes finding mine. "What're you doing back here?" His voice is laced with unfamiliar tension.

I pause, not so certain about my choice anymore. "Um, I was outside getting some fresh air and smelled the smoke and I..." I gulp down a nervous breath. "Are you okay?"

He nods, every muscle in his body wound tight. "I'm fine." He strains a smile, then grows silent, as if waiting for me to leave.

And maybe I should, just leave and give him some space. But I've spent so many years of my life pretending I was okay while deep down, wishing someone would see, see how much I was struggling and help me. Not that I would ever ask for it. Doing so would ruin the perfect image my mom wanted me to have. Would let everyone see my flaws. And at the time, I thought that was bad.

Now, though... Well, I'm not sure.

What I am sure about is that I don't want to leave Jett when he looks so broken.

"You're wearing fancy clothes," I state as I take in the short sleeved black button-shirt, and matching pants he's wearing.

He fiddles with the top button. "Yeah, this is about as fancy as I get. The other guys will probably have ties and vests on. Me..." He shrugs, lifting the joint to his lips and taking a hit. "I hate fancy clothes."

"My sister Alexis does too." I inch further into the alley-way, taking careful steps since my I'm barefoot and pebbles litter the area.

Smoke snakes from his lips as he leans back against the brick wall behind him and rests his arms on top of his knees. He has on a pair of black boots, the laces undone, and strands of his hair are sticking up everywhere.

"That doesn't surprise me," he says, staring at the wall across from him.

I dare another step closer to him and I'm within distance that the trail of smoke touches my nostrils. I should probably leave, but I can't bring myself to do so without making sure he's okay.

"You know her, right?" I step up beside him. "Alexis, I mean."

His gaze flits up to me and wariness floods his features. "Yeah," he tells me vaguely.

Maybe I'll regret asking him later, but right now I want to know... "How exactly?"

His wariness magnifies. "I'm not sure if I should tell you."

My brows narrow. "Why not?"

He wavers. "I don't know... I just don't want to get Alexis in trouble."

"I wouldn't tell on her. Besides, she's eighteen."

"True, but..." He lifts the joint to his lips. "I don't want you to think less of me either."

"And this will make me think that?"

"I don't know. I'm still trying to feel you out. I mean, back in the day, I would've said it would. But you're not what I expected."

"That seems to be a common thought with you guys," I mumble with a sigh.

He cracks a smile at that. "Someone else said that to you, huh?"

I nod. "Wilder said something similar."

"It's nothing personal. You just seem different from afar. Or maybe we're just corrupting you." He offers me a lopsided smile.

I smile back. "I don't think I'm corrupted."

His brow meticulously elevates. "So, I didn't see you downing a mimosa just a couple of minutes ago."

"I..." Does that mean I'm corrupted?

He lets out a soft laugh. "I'm just messing with you, Zhara." He shifts his weight, standing up and reclining against the wall. Then he nods for me to come closer to him. "I'll tell you about Alexis if you tell me one thing about you. I owe you one thing about me anyway."

Careful not to let the dress drag across the ground, I move over beside him and lean against the brick wall.

He doesn't speak right away, taking another hit, the last of the joint burning out. He drops it to the ground, the hitches his thumbs in his belt loops.

"I hung out with Alexis once. It was right after... Your parents died." He casts a cautious glance at me before continuing. "It was at a party that I technically wasn't supposed to be at because I was supposed to be working. I don't think she was supposed to be there either, but she was."

"It probably didn't matter if she was there," I inform him "Right after my parents died, no one was keeping an eye on anyone. All of us... my brothers and sisters... we were all just sort of wandering around, stuck in our own little worlds. Loki

—my older brother—had been told he had guardianship of us, but he still hadn't taken on the role of a parent yet... In the beginning, he was kind of a mess. We all were." Realizing I'm babbling, I shake my head. "Sorry. I didn't mean to pile all of that on you."

"You're fine," he assures me. "I kind of knew some of that already."

"How so?"

"Because that night I hung out with Alexis and we spent a lot of time... talking." He avoids my gaze, staring ahead.

"Just talking?" I question, because it seems like there might be more to the story than he's letting on.

Not that it's any of my business.

I'm about to tell him never mind, when he huffs out a frustrated exhale.

"I don't want you to hate me." He turns, facing me and resting his shoulder against the brick wall. "We're supposed to be on the same team and in order for everything to function properly within the team, there has to be very little drama. Not that there's not drama. There is, but we do our best to keep it at a minimum."

"You're fine. Whatever you say, I promise not to act over-dramatic." I toe at a pebble while staring at the ground. "Or if you don't want to tell me, you don't have to."

"No, it's fine..." His bloodshot eyes search mine. "I probably should tell you anyway or else there's going to be this secret between us and that's not cool." He shifts his weight, stuffing his hands into his pockets. "That night while we were hanging out, I was smoking, and she asked if she could have a hit. I didn't realize she'd never gotten high before until after I let her take one." He scratches at the back of his neck. "After that, she ended up drinking too much and got into this huge ass fight that led to her getting arrested. And... I don't know. I've always kind of felt responsible for that."

I remember that night. It was the first night Alexis was arrested, but wasn't the last. Loki hadn't known how to handle it. Luckily, the officer that had arrested her, knew our family, knew we had just lost our parents, and so he drove her home instead of to the station and let her off with a warning.

Maybe I should be irritated with Jett, though, for letting her get high, but I'm not. Not really. I've known for a while that my sister has done a lot of questionable things, and she's not innocent enough for me to blame it on anyone else. She's pretty blunt and doesn't give in to peer pressure. At least, that's who she became after our parents died. And it was her choice to do it, just like it's my choice to be here. I sometimes wonder why I am here

"It's not your fault. Alexis has always sort of done whatever she wanted to," I tell him. "And she never got in any real trouble for being arrested that night. The officer who arrested her knew us and just drove her home instead of taking her down to the station."

"Really?" he asks and I nod. "I always thought she was put on probation because of it. That's what I heard, anyway."

"She was put on probation later on, but not because of that incident. And I know that's not the only time she's gotten high. Or drunk. Or gotten into a fight." My chest rises and crashes as I blow out an exhale. "Alexis has gotten into a ton of trouble since my parents passed away."

"I'm sorry ... I know you say it's not my fault, but I still feel a bit guilty about what happened—Always have. I keep thinking if maybe if I'd told her no when she'd asked me to take that hit, she never would've done any of the rest of things that happened that night. Like I was the catalyst."

I don't want him to feel guilty about this. Yes, he may have given her the hit, but everything Alexis has done, she's chosen to do, and a lot of it, her pain was the catalyst. "I doubt it. Alexis has always been a bit wild and I think everything she's done has been her way of coping."

His head tilts to the side as he studies me. "You two are very different."

"Yeah, I get told that a lot." I lower my gaze to hide my frown.

He hooks his finger underneath my chin and lifts my gaze back to him. "That's not a bad thing, Zee."

A smile pulls at my lips.

"What?" Confused curiosity knits at his brows.

"It's nothing. You just called me Zee."

"Yeah, I did, didn't I?" He rubs his jawline musingly. "Maybe that can be my nickname for you."

"I'm fine with that, but I should probably tell you that Alexis calls me that sometimes."

He crinkles his nose. "Maybe I should come up with a more original one. Like Zee Bee. Or Hara. Of Zrharara."

I giggle. "That just sounds like a lot of noise."

"It does, doesn't it?" He wavers his head from side to side. "I think I'll just call you Zhara for now. It's a pretty name anyway."

"I'm okay with that."

"Cool."

We trade a smile, but his quickly morphs into wonderment. I want to ask him what's up, but he changes the subject.

"You know, I came out here to mentally prepare myself for

tonight because I always get a little bit nervous with these hardcore undercover roles," he informs me. "Usually, I take a few hits to calm myself down, and for the most part, it gets me to chill out, but you…" He points a finger at me. "You work much better."

"Um, thanks?" I say it more like a question. "I'm not sure how I helped, though."

"You're distracting." His bloodshot gaze skims across my face as he rubs his lips together. Then he straightens and removes his hands from his pockets. "So, as a thank you, I'm going to give you a few pointers for tonight."

"Bad girl pointers?"

"Maybe."

"Okay." What does that mean? When he settles into silence, I apprehensively add, "You're not going to make me sexy dance in this alleyway, are you?"

His lips kick up into a smirk. "What? Doesn't that sound fun?"

I peer around at the trash cans, the garbage everywhere, and the one-eyed, scraggly looking cat perched on the fence blocking the back of the alley. "I'm not sure any sort of dancing back here would be sexy."

He flicks his wrist, disagreeing. "Nah, when done right, you can sexy dance anywhere. But this is all a moot point anyway, because I'm not going to teach you how to sexy dance. I'm going to teach you how to be relaxed even when things seem intense. Which, I know, might sound ridiculous for me to be teaching you that since you just saw me trying to smoke the stress out of myself, but I do have other ways to get completely chillaxed."

"I appreciate the offer, but I'm not really a calm person. I wish I was, but I tend to get stressed out over things no matter what I do."

He crosses his arms and slants his head to the side. "See, I'm not buying into that. I know that's what everyone has told you you're like, but when that rogue unexpectedly broke into Benton's apartment, you handle the situation calmly, especially considering you've only been doing this undercover thing for like a week or so." He taps his finger against his lips. "Personally, I think you're gonna end up being the most badass of us all. But you still need some proper training, so here goes." He straightens his stance, popping his knuckles. "All right, first things first, we're going to do some breathing exercises."

"That kind of sounds nice, actually," I admit, thinking about how I was just wishing Jackson had taught me some.

But Jett can too.

"It is nice," he says. "I do this all the time, except I usually have a joint between my lips."

I attempt to smile back at his joke, but is it a joke?

I recall what Jackson said about Jett starting to get high all the time and how they're starting to get worried he has a problem. Not that I feel like it's my place to tell him. Yes, he's told me a couple of details about his past, but I still barely know him. So, I keep my lips zipped and mimic him as he breathes in and out.

The more inhales and exhales I take, the calmer I feel. That also might be because of the mimosa I drank. I'm not sure, though.

"Good," he says after he inhales and exhales. "Now do another."

I do as he says, letting oxygen in and out. "This feels nice."

"Yeah, it does," he murmurs, holding my gaze. "You and I should become breathing buddies."

I do another inhale and exhale. "Jackson already said him and I should be foot buddies."

He shrugs. "So? You can be foot buddies with him and breathing buddies with me."

I smile. "Okay."

He mirrors my smile, his lips parting, but the words fade from his tongue as his gaze drifts to something behind me. With the way he tenses, I half expect a rogue to be standing at the end of the alleyway.

But it's just Benton.

Benton all decked out in a back suit with a red tie.

Wow, he looks really nice in a suit. Like really, really *nice.*

Luckily, I keep that thought to myself to avoid looking like a spazz. Again.

His brows furrow as he takes in Jett and me. "What're you two doing back here?"

Jett lifts a shoulder, scuffing the tip of his boot against the ground. "I'm helping Zhara with some breathing exercises."

I'm highly aware that he doesn't mention he was stressed out before that happened. I'm not sure why he keeps this information from Benton—whether it's intentional or not—but I figure it's not my place to tell.

The crease between Benton's brow deepens as his gaze glides to me. "Are you nervous?"

"I don't know." I pick at the already chipped fingernail polish on my thumbnail. "Maybe a little. But the breathing exercises I did with Jett helped."

"I just want to make sure she feels relaxed," Jett adds, slipping his hands into his pockets. "It's important."

"I know." His gaze burrows into Jett, who avoids eye contact with him. Once he's done with dissecting Jett with his gaze, he focuses back on me. "I'm glad you're trying to relax, but the guys and I have come up with a plan that I think might make it so you don't have to talk to Drake, Tank, or Ralpho at all." He offers me his hand. "Come back into the store and I'll explain everything."

"Okay." I step forward and take his hand, hoping he's right.

Hoping he does have a plan.

Because while Jett's breathing exercises helped me for a moment, the feeling is already evaporating as I step out of the seclusion of the alleyway and back into the open space of the real world.

TWENTY-THREE
THE PROBABLY-NOT-SO LEGAL PLAN

WHEN WE GET BACK into the store, all of the guys are inside, lounging around on the sofa. Well, except for Ridge. They're all decked out in suits, button-down shirts, vests, ties. Also, lounging might not be the correct word since they all appear tense, their backs stiff, tension radiating off them.

"So what's this brilliant plan?" Jett asks as he flops down onto the chair and kicks his boots up onto the table.

Benton takes a seat on the edge of the table while I remain standing. With Wilder, Jackson, and Xavier all wedged on the longer sofa and Jett on the chair, there really is nowhere to sit.

"Are we good to talk?" Benton asks Xavier.

Xavier checks his phone. "Yeah, as long as the store owner doesn't come back."

"I sent her out on an errand," Wilder informs everyone. "I told her I needed a piece of jewelry that at this store clear across town, so she'll be a while."

"Good," Benton mutters, yanking his fingers through his

hair and making the strands go askew. "But just so everyone knows. My plan isn't brilliant. It just a plan."

"A plan that's going to come with a lot of consequences," Xavier stresses as he folds his arms across his chest. "Are you sure you want to do this?"

Benton doesn't answer right away. "I think it might be the only way."

"You better be sure. Not just think," Xavier throws back at him with a pressing look.

As they start to argue, Jackson crooks a finger at me and mouths, *"Come sit down."* Then he scoots over and pats the tiny spot between him and Wilder.

I pad over to him and wedge myself between them, uncertain what's going on, but somehow feeling like it's my fault. I begin to fidget, picking at my nail polish.

Jackson captures my hand. "Relax, cute girl. Everything's going to be okay now."

I glance at him. "Why do you say it like that? Like everything wasn't okay, but now it is."

"Because we made the decision to keep you away from the masquerade," Wilder tells me, his arm stretching out behind me and his fingers brushing through my hair.

My gaze darts to him, my eyes widening. *"What?"*

He offers me an edgy smile. "We decided it was too dangerous for you to go."

I look down at my dress then back at him. It doesn't make any sense. Why would they suddenly decide that I shouldn't go after they had made it seem so important that I did? What changed? Something had to.

"I don't understand." My gaze shifts between Jackson and

Wilder. "I thought I had to go... If I don't, won't that ruin your guys' cover?"

"We'll be fine," Jackson attempts to reassure me, but I detect the slight drop of doubt in his voice.

"No, we won't," Xavier says. When everyone gives him a dirty look, he scowls right back at them. "Look, I get why we're doing this, but everyone needs to realize there's going to be consequences if some of us just take off and bail out on this case."

"Take off?" I glance at the five of them, searching for an explanation.

At first, I think no one is going to give one to me, but then Jackson places a hand over mine.

"Remember how we were talking about traveling some-where?" he asks me, tracing the folds of my fingers with his fingertip.

I nod, trying not to shiver from his touch, but it feels good—soothing. "Yeah."

"Well, how would you feel about doing that now?" His fingers drift to the inside of my wrist.

It takes me a moment to process what he's saying. "Wait... You want to go to Scotland right now?"

"Not Scotland," Benton intervenes, scooting forward until his knees touch mine. "We're thinking London where your sister is. That way, you can have a good excuse for why you're going there. Plus, you'll have a family member close to you."

I wish I got why they're doing this. Why are they suddenly wanting to send me away? Why don't they want me to work with them anymore?

"Am I going to go alone?" I ask, my chest tighten.

I've never even flown before. Plus, I don't have a passport, clothes, anything really.

How the heck is this going to work?

Benton swiftly shakes his head then places his hands on my legs. "Jacks and Xavier are going to go with you. And eventually, some of your other team members might come over so we can switch places. It all really depends on how long you're over there."

I swallow down an uneven breath. "You don't know how long we're going for?"

"No," Benton answers reluctantly. "It all really depends on some stuff."

Stuff? What I vague word. All of this is vague.

And I want to ask for more details.

I should ask.

Just ask them, Zhara. Stop being the shy girl you've been programmed to believe you are.

"I just..." I sigh loudly. "I just don't get why we're going. Not that I won't go. I will if you think I need to. I just... I want to know why. And how? I mean, I don't have a passport. And don't you have to buy flight tickets like really early."

"Getting passports and tickets are the easy part—Ridge can handle all of that within a few hours. Although, we're going to have to give you an alias name so no one can track you down. Honestly, we probably should've done that from the beginning... We should've done a lot of things differently." Benton skims his fingers along my leg. "Look, I know this all sounds crazy, but with the rogues after you, we think it's better if you're some place far away where you'll be safe. I know it's a lot to ask—just taking off and trusting us—but we *need* you to trust us, sweetheart. Everything that we're doing is to protect you, with everything going on... trust is important."

Once again, I feel like I'm about to make a life-changing decision.

Trust them. Go to London with them. And without a clue as to how long I'll be there. Not to mention I'll have to think of something to tell Loki. Not that I don't already have some major explaining to do, but still.

And then there's the whole alias name, and Ridge being able to get me a passport within the hour. None of it sounds legal. Then again, should I even be worrying about that with everything else going on?

Think of the bigger picture, Zhara.

"I'll do it," I say softly, and I swear I feel them all visibly relax. "But what am I supposed to tell Loki?"

"You and Alexis were already coming up with a cover story anyway, so this can be it," Benton tells me, taking my free hand and holding it between his. "You can tell him that you and her, and maybe a couple of your friends are taking off on a trip. You don't need to tell him it's in London for now. That might seem a bit suspicious if you're able to just take off there without any planning. So, for now, you can tell him it's a road trip."

"A last minute trip road trip," Jackson adds, brushing some hair off my shoulder.

"That doesn't sound like me, though," I say. "At all."

"You could tell him about your list," Benton suggests.

"What list?" Xavier asks in confusion.

It reminds me that he'll be going to London with Jackson and me. I'm not sure why out of all the guys, he decided to go, since he doesn't like me very much. But maybe Benton is making him.

"That's between me and Zhara," Benton tells him while carrying my gaze. "If she wants to tell you, she can. But I'm not going to." He gives my hand a squeeze then stands to his feet. "Now, it's time to put this plan into motion. Jacks and Xav, take Zhara to her house so she can get packed. On the way, she can call Alexis. I recommend one of you talking to West or one of his team members to fill them in on what's going on. Ridge is already working on getting passports and flight tickets, so that is all taken care of. And you two," he glances at Wilder and Jett. "We have a party to attend."

"Why do we have to go to the party?" Jett gripes, begrudgingly. "And Jacks and Xav get to London. So not fair."

"Nothing ever is," Wilder tells him, briefly glancing at me before following Benton toward the front door.

"And why are we even going through with this anyway," Jett adds as he trudges along behind them. "Aren't we like bailing on this case?"

"We're not bailing on it," Benton replies as he pushes out the door.

He throws one last glance at me before exiting the store and a strange drop of emptiness creeps up on me.

But I quickly become distracted as Jackson stands up and offers me his hand. "You ready for an adventure, cute girl?"

He makes it sound so easy, but it's not.

I glance at Xavier, who's looking at me, but promptly looks away when our gazes collide. Then I look back at Jackson. Am I ready for this? Is it even an adventure? Honestly, it kind of feels like I'm running away from something.

Still, I place my hand in his and let Jackson pull me to my feet, deciding that maybe this isn't too terrible.

I mean, if I'm going to run from something, at least I have someone to run with me.

I just hope whatever we're running from doesn't end up catching us.

TWENTY-FOUR
BENTON

"ARE you sure this is the best option?" Wilder asks me after him, Jett, and I have piled into my car.

"For now, I think it is." I start up the engine. "After what Ridge found out, it's better that we get her out of here until we figure out what the fuck is going on."

And I'm not just referring to the assassination thing Ridge discovered. No, I'm also referring to the text I received from Ridge only minutes after he told me about Zhara possibly once being trained to become an assassin.

His text was simple, but sent a chill to my bones.

Ridge: I found out some more and it's bad. A guy named Drake is the one sending rogues after Zhara.

I'd replied with: *Our Drake? The one we're supposed to be meeting tonight? That Zhara is supposed to be meeting?*

He'd answered with a *I'm not sure. Either that or it's a guy that has the same name. But it's a very unsettling coincidence.*

And it was. It was also something I couldn't risk; the chance of it not being. So that was that. I knew Zhara couldn't go to that party, and that we needed to get her away from all of this.

So I came up with a quick plan, something I hate doing but seem to be doing a lot of lately. I'm going to tell Tank and Ralpho that Zhara and I broke up, so she no longer needs to go to the masquerade. There will be consequences for this, though, especially if their boss, Drake, is the one after Zhara. I mean, clearly tonight was a setup, but why? Why, if he's after her for some reason, has he not just pushed his way into her life already? Why does Zhara need to come to him? And why is he using rogues to go after her? A drug lord teaming up with rogues? It doesn't make any sense.

Just like it doesn't make sense that the Bosses car smelled like a drug experiment. And why did he want to talk to Zhara?

Why do I get the feeling that all of this is connected somehow?

"We're going to get into some serious trouble," Jett informs me. "You know that right."

I steer the car out of the parking space. "Of course, I do."

"Not just with Drake, but with Boss," he stresses. "We could even get kicked out of the program."

"I know," I say, gripping the wheel as anxiety threatens to creep through me.

"And you're not worried about that?" he questions.

I just shrug. The truth is I am worried. Really, really fucking worried. Not just about what's going to happen to us, but about something else Ridge found out while he was hacking into that chat room. Something I haven't told anyone yet, not because I want to lie to them, but because I don't know how to tell them.

That he tracked one of the chat room member's IP address

back to headquarters, which means someone inside might be working with Drake and the rogues. And again, I can't help thinking about how the Bosses car smelled like a drug experiment facility.

What if it's him?

What if no one is safe?

"Why are we going to this party anyway?" Wilder glances at me. "I mean, we're basically going rogue in our own way, so what's the point of even going through with this?"

"Because I want to find out more about this Drake," I inform him as I steer onto the road. "And this might be our only chance."

"That sounds dangerous," Wilder tells me, loosening the tie he's wearing.

"It probably is," I say with a shrug. "Everything we do is. But if you want to back out, you can. I won't force you to do anything."

He hesitates and then shakes his head. "No, I've got your back."

"Thanks." I glance at Jett in the rearview mirror. "What about you? Do you want to bail?"

He lets out a sigh then shakes his head. "You know I always have your back—we all do."

He's right. If there's one thing I know for sure in this world, it's that my team members will always have my back.

I just hope I'm taking care of them as well.

That I'm not leading them into some sort of trap.

But for the first time in an exceedingly long time, I'm not sure of anything anymore.

ABOUT THE AUTHOR

Jessica Sorensen is a *New York Times* and *USA Today* best-selling author who lives in the snowy mountains of Wyoming. When she's not writing, she spends her time reading and hanging out with her family.

ALSO BY JESSICA SORENSEN

<u>The Undercover Files:</u>

Meeting the Bad Boy Rebels

Bad Girl Training

Sweet Lies & Kisses

The Clock Tower & the Secret (coming spring 2020)

<u>Rebels & Misfits:</u>

Rules of a Rebels & a Shy Girl

<u>Enchanted Chaos Series:</u>

Enchanted Chaos

Charmed Chaos

Entangled Chaos

Untitled (coming soon)

<u>My Cursed Superhero Life:</u>

Cursed

Untitled (coming soon)

<u>Capturing Magic:</u>

Chasing Wishes

Chasing Magic

Chasing Promises

Untitled (coming soon)

<u>Chasing the Harlyton Sisters Series:</u>

Chasing Hadley

Falling for Hadley

Holding onto Hadley

Untitled (coming soon)

<u>Tangled Realms:</u>

Forever Violet

Untitled (coming soon)

<u>Curse of the Vampire Queen:</u>

Tempting Raven

Enchanting Raven

Alluring Raven

Untitled (coming soon)

<u>Unraveling You Series:</u>

Unraveling You

Raveling You

Awakening You

Inspiring You

Every Single Breath

Untitled (coming soon)

<u>**Unexpected Series:**</u>

The Unexpected Complications of Revenge

Untitled (coming soon)

Shadow Cove Series:

What Lies in the Darkness

What Lies in the Dark

Untitled (coming soon)

<u>**Mystic Willow Bay Series:**</u>

The Secret Life of a Witch

Broken Magic

Stolen Kisses

One Wild, Crazy, Zombie Night

Magical Whispers & the Undead

Untitled (coming soon)

<u>**Standalones:**</u>

The Forgotten Girl

<u>**The Fareland Society:**</u>

The Opposite of Ordinary

Untitled (coming soon)

<u>**Broken City Series:**</u>

Nameless

Forsaken

Oblivion

Forbidden (coming soon)

<u>Guardian Academy Series:</u>

Entranced

Entangled

Enchanted

Entice

The Forest of Shadow and Bones

Untitled (coming soon)

<u>Sunnyvale Series:</u>

The Year I Became Isabella Anders

The Year of Falling in Love

The Year of Second Chances

Untitled (coming soon)

<u>The Coincidence Series:</u>

The Coincidence of Callie and Kayden

The Redemption of Callie and Kayden

The Destiny of Violet and Luke

The Probability of Violet and Luke

The Certainty of Violet and Luke

The Resolution of Callie and Kayden

Seth & Greyson

The Evermore of Callie & Kayden

Untitled (coming soon)

The Secret Series:

The Prelude of Ella and Micha

The Secret of Ella and Micha

The Forever of Ella and Micha

The Temptation of Lila and Ethan

The Ever After of Ella and Micha

Lila and Ethan: Forever and Always

Untitled (coming soon)

Ella and Micha: Infinitely and Always

The Shattered Promises Series:

Shattered Promises

Fractured Souls

Unbroken

Broken Visions

Scattered Ashes

Breaking Nova Series:

Breaking Nova

Saving Quinton

Delilah: The Making of Red

Nova and Quinton: No Regrets

Tristan: Finding Hope

Wreck Me

Ruin Me

<u>The Fallen Star Series:</u>

The Fallen Star

The Underworld

The Vision

The Promise

The Lost Soul

The Evanescence

The Mist of Stars (untitled)

<u>The Darkness Falls Series:</u>

Darkness Falls

Darkness Breaks

Darkness Fades

<u>The Death Collectors Series (NA and YA):</u>

Ember X and Ember

Cinder X and Cinder

Spark X and Spark

<u>Unbeautiful Series:</u>

Unbeautiful

Untamed

Untamed